OCEAN OF BLOOD

THE SAGA OF LARTEN CREPSLEY: BOOK TWO

Other titles by
DARREN SHAN

* Also available on audio

DARREN SHAN

OCEAN OF BLOOD

THE SAGA OF LARTEN CREPSLEY: BOOK TWO

HarperCollins *Children's Books*

Darren Shan pilots his ship over the bloody waters of the internet at:
www.darrenshan.com

First published in hardback in Great Britain by HarperCollins *Children's Books* 2011

HarperCollins *Children's Books* is a division of HarperCollins*Publishers* Ltd
77-85 Fulham Palace Road, Hammersmith, London W6 8JB

Visit us at www.harpercollins.co.uk

Text copyright © Darren Shan 2011

ISBN 978-0-00-731588-8

Darren Shan reserves the right to be identified as the author of the work.

Typeset by Palimpsest Book Production Limited, Falkirk, Stirlingshire

Printed and bound in England by Clays Ltd, St Ives plc

For:
Shaun, Ciarán, Áine and Cian – monsters from the deep!

OBEs (Order of the Bloody Entrails) to:
Jessica Bromberg, the East Coast Kraken!!
Editorial Skipper: Sam Quint, AKA Nick Lake!!!
Admirals of the Dark Waters: Captain Christopher Little
and his scurvy crew!!!!

PART ONE

"a howling, hungry creature of dark delights"

CHAPTER ONE

The vampire known as Quicksilver threw a knife high into the smoke-clogged air of the tavern. Those around him watched with beady-eyed, bloodthirsty fascination as he held his head back, opened his mouth wide and waited for the knife to drop. A few people shrieked, but Quicksilver didn't flinch, expertly tracking the flight of the dagger. At precisely the right moment he clenched his teeth together and caught the blade two inches past the tip. As the handle quivered, he turned slowly, so that everyone in the room could see. Pulling out the knife, he threw it into the wood of the table – it drove in all the way to the hilt – and took a bow.

As the crowd went wild with applause, Quicksilver grinned and slumped into a chair close to another vampire and a gaggle of admiring young ladies. "There," he beamed. "I told you I could do it."

"One of these nights," the other bloodsucker said,

"you'll time that wrong and end up with a knife through the back of your throat."

"Don't be such an old woman, Wester," Quicksilver laughed. "You'll scare these lovely creatures and I would hate to send them to bed with nightmares."

"It will take more than your dull tales to scare *us*," one of the ladies snorted, but they were undeniably impressed.

"What's your real name?" another lady asked, cuddling up to the man with the odd, orange hair, immaculate grey suit and dazzling smile.

"I only reveal that to my *very* special friends," Quicksilver murmured. Then, as she blushed, he whispered in her ear, "Larten Crepsley." After that he called for more wine and the rest of the night passed most pleasantly.

A groggy Wester rose before Larten and stumbled to the window of the inn where they had bedded for the day. He peered through the curtains at the sunlight, hissed and let them swish shut. It would be another couple of hours before they could go out. The sun wouldn't kill the vampires instantly, but they'd start to redden within minutes and would be in agony in less than an hour. If they were exposed to its rays for two or three hours, there would be nothing left of them except for charred bones.

Wester washed in a basin of water and studied his beard in the mirror above it. Shaving was a complicated business for vampires. Normal razors were useless on their tough hair. He and Larten had picked up specially hardened blades a couple of years ago, but Wester had lost his in the course of their travels. He'd asked to borrow Larten's, but the slightly older vampire had said it was time Wester learnt to take better care of his possessions. Larten had just been teasing him, but Wester didn't want to give his friend the satisfaction of seeing him plead, so he'd grown a beard since then.

"My head," Larten groaned, sitting up, then flopping back again. "What time is it?"

"Too early to be getting up," Wester grunted.

"How much did we drink last night?"

"I don't want to think about it."

Vampires could consume a lot more alcohol than humans and it was difficult for them to get drunk. But Wester and Larten had been managing to defy the physical odds most nights.

"They were nice ladies," Larten chuckled. "They loved my knife trick."

"You should try it at the Cirque Du Freak," Wester said drily. "It would go down a treat there."

The pair had bumped into their old ally, Mr Tall, a while ago. They'd spent a fun few nights with the circus crew and Larten had performed some of his old magic routines in the show. He had been rusty to begin with, but adjusted swiftly. He had an incredibly fast hand, even for a vampire. It was how he'd earned his nickname — one of their friends had once said his fingers moved as if made of quicksilver.

Larten and Wester had been travelling the world for almost twenty years since their first time at Council. Both had learned a lot, not just about the ways of vampires, but about ladies too. Larten had been a slow starter, but was making up for lost time, dazzling maidens with his smile, confidence and agility wherever he went.

The pair occasionally met with their master, Seba Nile, but spent most of the time by themselves or with others their age, vampires in their thirties, forties, fifties or sixties. They were youths by vampire standards and had been cut loose by their masters to explore the world of humans one final time before pledging themselves to the demands of the clan.

The door to their room crashed open. Wester whirled defensively, then relaxed as a large vampire with long blond hair staggered in. It was Yebba. He had been travelling with them for the past month, though it had been a few nights since they'd last seen him.

"I'm thirsty," Yebba roared, kicking Larten's bed. "Up, cur, and come keep me company."

"Wester says the sun hasn't set yet," Larten yawned.

"I don't give a damn," the massive vampire said, then collapsed like a bear and sat on the floor, blinking dumbly.

"A heavy night's drinking?" Wester smiled.

"Aye," Yebba said morosely. "A woman broke my heart. What else could I do but drown my sorrows in ale?"

"Another broken heart?" Wester tsked. "That must be the fourth this year."

"Aye." Tears welled in Yebba's eyes. "Vampires weren't made for love."

"What happened this time?" Wester asked slyly. "Did you bite her?"

"That only happened once," Yebba scowled. "And it was an accident."

"It has happened to us all," Larten said, propping himself on an elbow.

"I don't remember you biting any of your lady friends," Wester frowned.

"No, but there was one time…" He coughed and blushed. "Never mind."

"Tell us," Wester hooted. "Come on, *Quicksilver*, you can't leave Yebba to bare his soul alone."

"Well, do you recall a night a couple of years ago when I didn't return to our inn?"

"That happens at least once a month," Wester said.

"This was different," Larten snapped. "I'd been out with a lady and drank more than was good for me. I felt hungry on the way home, so I popped into a room to feed. But I made too much noise and woke the woman up. She screamed blue murder and I tumbled out of her room without silencing her."

"Why didn't you breathe on her and knock her out?" Wester asked.

Larten shrugged. "I was drunk. I forgot about my vampiric breath. Before I knew it, a mob had formed and I was chased out of town. I was almost trapped in the open and burnt alive."

When Wester and Yebba had stopped laughing, Yebba said, "Why didn't you flit? They couldn't have troubled you once you hit top speed and vanished from sight."

Larten's blush deepened and Wester had to answer for him. "He can't flit when he's drunk — he loses his sense of coordination and can't run that fast."

The pair fell apart with laughter. Larten sniffed angrily, but his lips were twitching at the corners. Eventually he burst out laughing too. When their fit had passed, Wester trudged down to order food and ale, then the three of them waited for the sun to set, so that they could again seek excitement in the inns, taverns and gaming halls of the humans they had once been.

CHAPTER TWO

After a few drinks downstairs, the three young vampires went in search of whatever pleasures they could find. They were adept at sniffing out all of the hidden delights of a town.

The trio gained admittance to a boxing match that they enjoyed greatly, wagering heavily on the outcome. Vampires usually didn't bother with money, but Cubs often stole from sleeping humans when they fed. Superstitious people thought that vampires were fanged beasts who ripped open the throats of their targets. In reality they normally slipped into a bedroom, made a small cut on the arm or leg of a sleeping human, drank just enough blood to sate their hunger, then used their spit to close the wound.

Larten studied the scars on his fingertips during a rest between rounds. He had been blooded the traditional way. Seba sliced the tips of Larten's fingers with his hard, sharp nails, then cut his own and pumped blood into his assistant. Larten was proud of the scars, though sometimes when he studied them he felt a stab of guilt. They reminded him of Seba and he wondered what his master would think of his student's recent behaviour.

Larten and Seba had parted on bad terms, but had made their peace since then. Larten worried that by gambling, drinking and stealing, he and Wester were soiling their master's good name. Wester often had to remind him (especially when Larten had drunk too much and was in a maudlin mood) that Seba had told them to work their human interests out of their system. There were lots of other vampires going through the same thing. They were called Cubs by the older members of the clan.

The fight recommenced and the burly men closed in on one another. Larten looked up from his fingers and focused on the boxers. This was the thirty-second round and it had been a long time since he'd seen so engaging a battle. He cheered on the stout-hearted warriors as they clashed, weary and unsteady on their feet, but determined to keep going.

The flesh of their bare fists had been torn to pieces and blood splattered every time one of them landed a blow. The ruby-red drops made Larten's mouth water – Wester and Yebba were staring hungrily too – and he had to warn himself to stay by the side, not dart forward and latch on to the delicious wounds.

All around, men were betting and roaring encouragement or abuse. They all had the same greedy, heated look in their eyes.

"My one's winning," Yebba whooped as one of the brutes landed a blow.

"You didn't bet on him," Wester retorted. "You bet on the other one."

"Did not!" Yebba shouted.

"Yes you did. He has that mark on his left arm, remember?"

Yebba squinted at the boxers, then cursed. "These humans all look the same to me," he growled. Larten and Wester laughed and passed the disgruntled vampire another mug of ale — that was guaranteed to settle him down.

After the fight, Larten and Wester collected their winnings and took Yebba to a tavern where they found ladies to dance with. Small towns lacked the dance halls of big cities, but you could always sort out something if you splashed enough money around.

They joined a card game later. All three were drunk and they lost heavily, even Larten, who rarely tasted defeat at the gambling tables. But they didn't mind.

Money was easy to come by if you were a creature of the night.

Larten wanted to do his knife-catching trick again, but Wester wouldn't let him. He took his friend's knife away and held it out of reach as Larten tried to snatch it back. If they had been sober, Wester couldn't have kept it from the faster, stronger vampire. But Larten was woozy and helpless. Wester had a knack of knowing when Larten was going to drink more than he could handle, and he stayed relatively clear-headed on those nights so that he could keep an eye on his reckless friend.

"Ish not fair," Larten complained to a man with a monocle. "I'm Qui-*hic*! I'm Quick-*hic*!" He gulped ale until the hiccups went away. "I'm Quicksilver," he growled majestically.

"Aye?" the man said, passing Larten a pinch of snuff. "I'm in the leather trade myself."

"Not my bizzzness," Larten slurred. "Ish my… ish my…" He pulled a face and forgot what he was trying to say, then fell face down on the table and knew no more until morning.

Larten awoke to savage pain. He was outside in the sun and his skin was a nasty red shade. As he blinked sleep from his eyes and tried to raise a hand to protect his face from the rays, he found that his arms were tied behind his back and he was hanging upside down. His shirt had been ripped away, exposing his torso, which had been burnt as deeply as his face.

Fear flared in his heart, but he thrust it from his thoughts. He didn't know what was going on — perhaps he had been caught feeding drunkenly — but that didn't matter. He had to escape quickly or he would burn like a pig on a spit.

Larten set to work on the knots around his wrists. He was hanging from a thick length of rope, swinging and turning in a soft breeze, but he ignored that and kept as still as possible, except for his fingers, which danced over the knots. The long, hardened nails of the vampires were invaluable when it came to picking knots and locks, but Larten would have been able to make short work of these regardless. He had learnt well from Merletta all those years ago.

Once his hands were free, he wriggled loose of the ropes binding his arms and chest. Bending upwards, he grabbed the supporting rope with one hand, tore apart the ropes around his legs with the other, hung in the air a moment, then dropped to his feet and landed in a crouch. His first instinct was to dart for the safety of the shadows, but he forced himself to scan the doorways of the sheds around him — he was in a courtyard – looking for the enemies who had strung him up.

For long, anxious seconds, Larten searched for his foes and readied himself for battle. Then he caught a scent and his nose crinkled with disgust. He rose and brushed dirt from his trousers. He dug out his watch and checked the time – it was for show, as Seba had taught him to read the time based on the position of the sun and stars – then coolly glanced at the sky and sniffed.

"My watch has stopped, Tanish," he called. "If it's broken, I'll have the price of a new one out of you."

Laughter greeted this statement and four vampires lurched out of a shed. One was a sheepish-looking Wester Flack. The others were Yebba, Zula Pone and Tanish Eul, the vampire who had originally given Larten his nickname.

"The same old Quicksilver," Tanish snorted admiringly, then hurried forward to throw a cloak over the head and shoulders of his friend and bundle him into the shadows of the shed where a barrel of ale was waiting.

CHAPTER THREE

Tanish Eul was tall and thin, with a stunning smile and carefully groomed hair and nails. He was always stylishly dressed, and spoke in the smooth tones of a silver-tongued rogue. If Larten was a Romeo, Tanish was a full-blown Casanova — his success with the ladies was legendary.

Zula Pone, on the other hand, was one of the shortest people Larten had ever met. He was stout and ugly. Many vampires were rough by human standards, their faces laced with scars and patches from old wounds, but they were considered fair among their own. Poor Zula was ugly by any reckoning. Fortunately he didn't care, and even wore shabby clothes and cut his hair crookedly to prove he was immune to what others thought of his looks. Despite this, Zula was a surprise hit with those of the fairer sex. He generally repulsed them to begin with, but after ten minutes in his company virtually any woman found herself won over by his charm.

Tanish had run into Zula a few years ago and instantly recognised a kindred spirit. They'd become fast friends and it wasn't long before Larten and Wester were introduced to the newest member of their rowdy pack.

"You've got fairer skin than a baby," Tanish hooted as Larten rested in the shed and tried not to move — his burnt flesh sent needles shooting through him every time he shifted. "You were only up there half an hour. I'd be a mild pink colour if it had been me."

"You'll be red with your own blood if you ever try that again," Larten said angrily. "What if I hadn't been able to undo the knots?"

"We were keeping a close watch on you," Wester said. "We would have seen if you were in trouble."

"And left you there to burn!" Zula exploded.

Larten found himself laughing along with the others. It had been a good joke, even though he was the butt of it. Wester was the only one who couldn't see the funny side. He smiled along with the rest of them, but his smile was strained. Larten would be tender for the coming week, his flesh would peel and some of the sores might fester. Wester saw nothing humorous in that.

The vampires drank and chatted for a few hours, telling tall and bawdy tales. Tanish and Zula had been involved in a number of near scrapes as usual and had been run out of the last three towns they'd visited.

"The problem with humans is that they take life too seriously," Tanish sneered. "Admittedly, we burnt down a storehouse with a winter's supply of grain in it, so a few children will go hungry this year. So what? It will sort out the strong from the weak. Humans are too attached to their young. The vampaneze have the right idea — humans are only fit for killing."

Tanish winked at Larten as he said that, then looked as innocent as he could when Wester flared up. "That's a horrible thing to say! We were the same as them before we were blooded. They have shorter lives than us and are much weaker. If we kill humans, we disgrace ourselves. The vampaneze are soulless scum who will never find Paradise, and more fool you if you can't see that."

Wester ranted for another fifteen minutes. His hatred of the vampaneze had set in him like a disease, and though he spoke little of the matter most of the time, those close to him knew of his true feelings. Seba had tried reasoning with him — just because a vampaneze had killed his family, it didn't mean he should hate all of them — but Wester refused to listen.

Wester's hatred of the breakaway group of night-walkers troubled Larten more than it worried Seba.

Their master had seen this dark bent in Wester many decades before and was convinced the young vampire would meet an early end at the hands of one purple-skinned vampaneze or another. But Larten had always hoped that Wester would come to terms with his loss and put his hatred behind him.

Larten had urged his dearest friend to track down Murlough – the one who had slain Wester's family – and kill him. He thought that would finally help Wester to put that dark night behind him. But Wester was reluctant to do that. He had come to hate the entire vampaneze clan. He sometimes swore that he would finish off Murlough only when he was done with the rest of the scum, that he wanted his foe to suffer the same kind of loss that Wester had been forced to endure.

Tanish shrugged when Wester finally lapsed into a fuming silence. "The vampaneze mean nothing to me," he said. "If war breaks out between us, I'll fight them and be glad of the challenge. But as long as the truce is in place, what do they matter?"

"Desmond Tiny would beg to differ," Wester growled. "He said the vampaneze would unite behind a mighty leader one night, that their Lord would lead them into war with us and wipe us from the face of the Earth."

"I've never seen the legendary Mr Tiny and I don't believe he's as powerful as certain old fools claim," Tanish said dismissively.

"Seba saw him," Larten said softly. "He was at Vampire Mountain when Tiny visited after the vampaneze split from the clan. Seba heard him make his prophecy. *He* takes it seriously."

Desmond Tiny was a being of immense magical power, who had predicted the downfall of the clan at the hands of the vampaneze. Lots of younger vampires thought he was a mythical creature. Larten might have too if his master hadn't told him of the night when Mr Tiny visited the vampire base. He had seen the fear in Seba's eyes, even all these centuries later.

"When I was blooded," Larten continued, "Seba made me hold on to the Stone of Blood for longer than necessary. He said that the Stone was our only hope of thwarting destiny. Mr Tiny gave us the Stone to give us hope. Tiny craves chaos. He doesn't want the vampaneze to eliminate us too easily. He'd rather we get dragged into a long war full of suffering and torment."

Larten stared again at the marks on his fingers, remembering the night when he had embraced the Stone of Blood and surrendered himself forever to the rule of the clan.

"I didn't mean to belittle Seba Nile," Tanish said,

choosing his words with care. He wasn't close to his own master, but he knew Larten respected Seba. "If he says he saw Desmond Tiny, I believe him and apologise if I offended you."

Larten made light of Tanish's apology, though secretly it made him uneasy. He could feel himself starting to drift away from Tanish and the Cubs. Larten was growing tired of the endless drinking, gambling and womanising. He wasn't yet ready to turn his back on the human world and its many delights, but he was sure he would return to Seba in a few more years to resume his studies.

He doubted Tanish would abandon the easy life so willingly. Some Cubs ended up rejecting the ways of the clan. They grew attached to human comforts and chose to remain in that soft, safe world. The Generals allowed them their freedom so long as they obeyed certain laws. Larten thought that Tanish would be one of those who never returned to Vampire Mountain, but wandered forever among humans.

"Enough of the damn vampaneze," Zula scowled. "A pox on their purple skin. We have more important matters to discuss."

"Such as?" Larten asked, a twinkle in his eyes, anticipating the answer.

"A war pack has formed." Zula licked his lips and

grinned. "They're no more than a night's march from here."

"We thought we'd swing by for you two in case you were interested," Tanish said.

"You thought right," Larten chuckled. "We'll set off at dusk."

"With your skin as red as a lobster's?" Wester asked.

"A minor irritation," Larten said, wincing as he leant back on his bed of straw.

Without any further discussion he closed his eyes. The others lay down and also prepared for sleep, though it would be a long time before any of them dozed. They rested in the shade for much of the morning, eyes closed but awake, thinking of the war pack, stomachs rumbling with excitement... and hunger.

CHAPTER FOUR

War was the great addiction of humans. Vampires loved to fight and got involved in bloody, brutal challenges all the time. But they had only been involved in a war once, when seventy of their clan broke away to become the vampaneze. Although various vampires had clashed with human forces in the past, they had never engaged in all-out conflict. As an old pun put it, war was not in their blood.

Humans, on the other hand, seemed to be interested in nothing else. Larten had seen much of the globe in the last twenty years. He had explored the continents of Europe, Africa, America and Asia. Wars raged everywhere as men found new, inventive ways to kill even more of their race. It was like a contest, the many tribes of mankind competing to see who could commit the worst atrocities.

Although mature vampires were not drawn to war, the Cubs were fascinated by it. To them it was a spectator sport, the same as boxing or wrestling. Many met at battlefields and cheered on the soldiers, laughed at the innocents trying to escape the crossfire, gambled on who would claim victory.

And of course they fed. By the gods, how they fed!

The war which Larten and his associates travelled to observe that night was a minor skirmish. Scholars might recall it in later decades, but it would not be marked as one of the important battles of its time. No vast chunks of land were at stake. History didn't hang in the balance. There were no real profits to be made. It was just one more clash of men who felt driven to kill each other for reasons only their leaders knew. And sometimes not even their kings and generals could explain why they were fighting. They often went to war simply because they could think of nothing else to do.

The vampires arrived a few hours before dawn. Signs of fighting were everywhere — bloodstained fields, discarded swords and muskets, limbs that had been left to rot, even a few whole bodies. There was a foul stench and the animals and birds of the night were gorging themselves, picking flesh from bones and nibbling on guts, making the most of the unexpected feast.

Tanish studied a field of trampled crops. His sharp

eyes picked out the corpse of a child among the broken stalks. The head of a soldier was half submerged in a rabbit hole. A bare foot was sticking up into the air — the four small toes had been chewed off, leaving only the big toe pointing oddly at the sky. Tanish ran his gaze over the blood and entrails, taking it all in.

Then he laughed.

"These look like an especially vicious lot," Tanish said enthusiastically. "We should have an interesting day."

"You don't think we've missed all the fighting?" Zula asked.

"Not by a long shot," Yebba said. "I smell human fear in the air. That way." He pointed west. "And there." East. "They mean to clash again and they know many more will die when they do."

Although Larten could smell the soldiers, he wasn't able to pinpoint the scent of fear. But Yebba was fifteen years older and had been blooded when he was only thirteen. A vampire's senses improved for most of their first hundred years.

The sharp-nosed Yebba led the way as they homed in on their kin. Vampires were harder to track than humans. If Larten hadn't known there were others present, he probably wouldn't have noted the subtle traces of their smell in the air.

31

They found the war pack resting beneath a massive, leafy tree. There were eight of them, a couple younger than Larten, the rest the same age as him or older. Tanish was the eldest and he immediately acted as if he was the ranking vampire.

"On your feet, you lazy, good-for-nothing Cubs," he snarled, standing just beyond the limbs of the tree, glaring like a General. "Is this any way to behave in front of your betters?"

"You're no better than the pimples on my backside, Tanish," a vampire drawled. Larten recognised him — Jordan Egin, one of three in the pack that he'd met before.

Jordan rose, slouched towards Tanish, sneered in his face, then laughed and hugged him hard. "Good to see you again, old friend."

"And you," Tanish beamed. "You'll remember these two."

"Larten and Wester," Jordan nodded. "We feasted heartily last time, aye?"

The pair chuckled at the memory, although Wester looked somewhat ashamed. He had overindulged on that occasion and been violently sick afterwards.

"These are Yebba and Zula Pone," Tanish said. "Yebba has a nose like a hound and Zula is a villain of the highest order. You'll get on well."

The vampires shook hands, then moved forward to greet the rest of the pack. It wasn't long before they were guzzling ale and swapping tales of their adventures.

War packs were a relatively new phenomenon. Vampires had tended to stay out of the way of warring humans in the past, not drawing attention to themselves. But there were so many wars being fought now, on such a massive scale, that the night-walkers could mingle freely with human troops in most places. The Cubs had started frequenting battlefields several decades earlier and now it was a common part of their lives. A lone vampire could nearly always be assured of finding company in a war zone.

Larten listened happily to the stories of Jordan and the others, and told some of his own in return. There was much laughter when Tanish told them of the trick he had played the previous night, and Larten had to take off his jacket and shirt to show his sunburnt back. He had already recovered from the worst of the burning, but his skin was still sore to the touch and a few of the vampires slapped him and hooted when he screeched. He had to knock a couple of heads together before they left him alone, but it was all done in good spirits.

The next bout between the armies wasn't due to

33

start until late in the morning — both sides were waiting for fresh recruits. So the pack turned in when the sun rose and caught some sleep. When they were awakened by the sound of gunfire, they groaned, stretched, took umbrellas from a large sack and set off to find the battle.

Larten had felt foolish the first time he'd stood by a group of soldiers hellbent on killing one another, sheltered from the sun beneath an umbrella that would have suited a lady far better. But he had grown accustomed to it. He now felt the same way a huntsman did when he pulled on ridiculous-looking clothes before mounting his horse and riding out behind his hounds.

The Cubs found the soldiers massed in a large field. They were fighting hand to hand. Most were armed with swords or knives, which the vampires preferred. They disliked guns for a number of reasons, firstly because the clan frowned on the use of them — guns were the choice of cowards. There was also the fact that guns could be turned against the Cubs. Vampires were tougher than humans and much harder to kill, but a well-placed bullet could account for even the best of them. It was an embarrassing way to die, your brains blown out from a distance.

But mostly the Cubs disapproved of long-range

warfare because it was boring. There wasn't much fun in watching humans shoot each other. The delight came in observing them struggle to stay alive. In dirty scraps like this, dozens of duels were being fought, life-or-death dramas which the vampires could follow with ghoulish glee, then turn away from at the end and discuss like a play.

Some of the soldiers noticed the curious men with the umbrellas, but most were too focused on the business of staying alive. If they caught sight of the scarred, pale-skinned figures walking among them, they paused to assess whether or not the strangers posed a threat. When the soldiers saw that the observers meant them no harm, their attention returned to those who did.

The vampires were almost never challenged. Humans who spotted them didn't always know who the spectators were – many had never heard the vampire myths – but they could tell that the guests were not of their own kind. They would watch the wan creatures gliding through their ranks, neatly stepping out of danger's way whenever they got too close to the action. Sometimes the soldiers would cross themselves and mutter prayers. But the majority chose not to confront the spectral visitors and did their best to forget about them if they survived. There were things in the world that most people didn't want to dwell on at any great length.

Larten had a fine time that day. As Tanish had predicted, the armies fought with a vengeance. Whatever they were warring over, the troops clearly hated their opponents and were determined to shed as much blood as possible before a truce was declared. They didn't just stab one another and move on. When a soldier knocked down a foe, he paused to strike again, gutting his opponent, smashing his face to pieces, often maiming him even after he was dead. It was a savage, bloodthirsty display, very much to Larten's liking.

Occasionally, when straddling corpses and wading through puddles of blood, Larten would remember that he had once been human. If his life hadn't taken the turn it did, he might have wound up on a field like this, fighting to the death, killing because he had to. He'd wonder how he would have felt in that position if he had looked up and seen a vampire studying him like an insect.

Larten always pushed such thoughts swiftly from his head. One of the hardest things about being a vampire was separating yourself from your origins. You had to leave behind your old ways to truly fit into the clan. There was no room for pity if you wanted to become a vampire of good standing. You had to force yourself to see humans as a different, lesser species.

A young man was shot in the shoulder and spun around from the force of it. He fell against Larten, who steadied him with one hand, keeping his umbrella straight with the other. The man's eyes widened with fear and wonder. Then the pain kicked in and he doubled over. Larten nearly bent to help him, but if he showed favouritism the soldiers of the other army might fire on him. Both sets ignored the vampires because they were neutral. If they interfered, they risked drawing fire. So Larten left the young man to writhe in the dirt, lonely and untended, and strolled along.

The battle lasted most of the afternoon. The war pack withdrew in the evening to rest. They debated the highlights, each reporting on what he had witnessed. A few had been cut or struck, and Jordan had been shot in his left arm. But the wounds weren't serious and they laughed about them as they relaxed beneath a tree, comparing scratches.

The vampires dozed, letting the sun drop. When darkness had settled on the world, they returned to the killing zone. There were no smiles this time, or if there were, they were tight, vicious, inhuman sneers. No banter either. They proceeded smoothly and silently.

The umbrellas were left behind and when they reached the edge of the battlefield they shed their coats, cloaks and boots. A couple even stripped naked, baring all beneath the moon.

For a minute they stood on the flanks, drinking in the sight of the corpses and mouthwatering pools of blood. No humans moved. Even those who'd never heard of vampires had sensed menace in the night air and withdrawn to the safety of camp. In the morning they would return to bury the bodies of their fallen allies and pick weapons, shoes and other items from the dead. But the night belonged to the Cubs.

When the vampires were satisfied that the field was theirs, they closed in. Each trod softly, barely trampling the grass as they advanced on the corpses. Their nostrils and eyes were wide. Drool dripped from the lips of many. Some trembled with expectation. Others growled softly.

They held as a pack until they were in the middle of the slaughter. Then all eyes settled on Tanish. Though they had scorned his claims of leadership earlier, in this situation they acknowledged his right to command. If he hesitated, they would ignore him and press on, but they gave him the chance to unleash them, as was the vampire way.

Tanish beamed wolfishly, then snapped his teeth

and threw himself on to all fours. Around him the others did the same. Breaking away from one another, they dug into the bodies of the slain, slicing flesh from bone, gulping blood as it gushed into the air, wallowing in the thick, red liquid.

After a while they started to howl and beat the ground with bones which they had snapped loose. Some fought with each other, wrestling clumsily, but the fights didn't last long. They could challenge one another for real any time. These ripe nights were reserved for pleasures more savage than battle.

Like the rest of his pack, Larten soon lost himself in the feeding frenzy. For an hour or more he was neither human nor vampire, just a howling, hungry creature of dark delights. At times he slithered across the cool, sticky bodies like a ravenous worm, cutting, chewing, drinking. And all he knew… all any of them knew… all that their world consisted of in that intense, vicious, darkly delicious time… was *blood*.

CHAPTER FIVE

The vampires slept late the following day. A couple rose to observe the fighting in the afternoon, but most had seen enough and preferred to rest, digest their feast and dream of future feeding frenzies.

"Wake up," Tanish grunted in the evening, digging Larten in the ribs.

"Leave me alone," Larten growled.

"You've slept enough," Tanish said. "I'm bored. I want you to teach me some new tricks."

"Have you mastered the ones I taught you last time?"

"Some of them." Tanish laughed. "I'm quite good at those that I can use when playing poker."

"You cheat when you gamble?" Larten frowned, sitting up.

"If I need money." Tanish shrugged. "I don't like to steal. I'd rather work for my ill-gotten gains."

"You think cheating is work?"

"We're only talking about humans," Tanish said. "I'd

never scheme against one of our own. Come on, Quicksilver, you love to show off. You've the fastest hands I've ever seen. Teach me, o wise and nimble-fingered one."

Larten smiled and took a pack of cards from a small, leather bag. He shuffled for a couple of minutes to limber up, then taught Tanish a few new ways to make the cards do whatever he wished. He had to slow down his movements so that his friend could follow.

"You're unnatural," Tanish said admiringly. "Are you this fast in a fight?"

"You've seen me fight many times," Larten said.

"Drunken skirmishes, yes, but never in a real battle. Have you ever fought to the death?"

Larten shook his head. "Not since I was blooded."

"You mean you killed before?"

"I don't want to talk about it."

"Oh-ho! Quicksilver's hiding a secret. Tell me. I won't leave you in peace until you do."

"This is not a topic for discussion," Larten said softly, and although there was no menace in his tone, Tanish knew immediately that the orange-haired vampire was serious. He snorted as if he didn't care, then focused on the cards.

As they played and the others stirred around them,

a man approached across one of the fields of carnage. He was moving faster than a human, sheltered beneath a heavy cloak. Larten assumed it was another Cub coming to join the pack. The newcomer would be disappointed — by the diminished sounds of battle, it seemed that the soldiers had spent the worst of their anger. The war was winding down.

The man slowed when he spotted the vampires under the tree. He studied them, his face masked by the shadows cast by his cloak. Then he came forward. When he was at the edge of the tree's reach, he let his cloak drop.

"By the black blood of Harnon Oan!" Wester roared, leaping to his feet, gawping at the stranger with disbelief.

The newcomer was no human, but he wasn't a vampire either. He had light red hair and fingernails, a pair of burning red eyes, and his skin was a purplish shade.

"I am Randel Chayne of the vampaneze," he said as the rest of the Cubs leapt up like the shocked Wester. "I come to seek a challenge."

Nobody spoke. They were astonished. Challenges between the two tribes of the night were nothing new, but Cubs were normally ignored in favour of Generals. This was the first time most of them had seen one of their estranged blood-cousins.

Randel studied the dumbstruck vampires, his eyebrows arching. "If this is how vampires react in the face of a challenge, perhaps you are not worth fighting."

"We'll teach you about *worth*, you scum!" Wester screamed, lunging at the vampaneze, hands twisted into claws, hatred darkening his features.

Larten grabbed his friend and held him back. "No," he snapped. "You're not ready for this. He'll kill you."

"Let me go," Wester snarled as Randel laughed cruelly. "You have no right to get in my way. I'll rip his throat open, and if you try to stop me, I'll—"

"He'll break your neck before you can lay a hand on him," Larten said coldly. "He's not an assistant, you can tell by the dark colour of his skin. He's a full vampaneze. He must be a vampire-hater or he wouldn't have bothered with Cubs like us. He's not looking for a challenge — he just wants to rack up an easy kill.

"That's it, isn't it?" Larten shouted at the vampaneze. "You don't dare face one of our Generals, so you hunt among the inexperienced Cubs. You're a coward."

Randel sneered. "I've fought and killed Generals, and one night I will fight and kill a Prince if the gods are good to me. I have nothing to prove and I don't react to the insults of curs like you. But today, to pass the time, I want to face a Cub. I've been told you're slow and soft. Can any of you prove me wrong?"

Wester's eyes flashed and again he tried to strike. Larten blocked him and said without emotion, "If you fight, he'll slay you and you'll never be able to take revenge on the one who murdered your family." Then he stood aside, letting Wester make the final decision, as was his right.

As Wester agonised – he wanted more than anything to kill the stranger, but he knew Larten spoke truly – Randel gazed with disgust at the war pack. "Surely you have a leader," he teased. "Vampires love to be led. Will not even the mighty pack leader meet my challenge?"

All eyes turned to Tanish. He had demanded the right to rule and they'd granted it. If he didn't meet this challenge, he would be disgraced. Any vampire of good standing in his position must step forward. Even the wayward Cubs had standards to uphold. The members of the pack expected Tanish to face this purple-skinned villain, put up a good fight and die with honour.

But Tanish didn't move. His cheeks were burning and he stared at the ground as if he could never look up again. When they realised he wasn't going to react, their faces hardened. Several puffed themselves up for battle – even the wounded Jordan struggled to his feet – but Zula Pone was the first to step forward.

"I will face you, Randel of the vampaneze," Zula

said, taking off the overcoat in which he had been sleeping. "And when I kill you, I will honour your corpse and say a prayer to the vampire gods to accept your wayward soul."

Randel laughed, but the sneering tone was gone from his voice when he said, "I accept your challenge. But I'll not ask for your name or make pleas on your behalf to the gods when this is over. That's not our way. We simply kill or die. The glory lies in the battle, not what is said or done afterwards."

Randel edged away from the shelter of the tree, into the deadly sunlight. Like vampires, he couldn't comfortably stand exposure to the sun. But fights between children of the night seldom lasted more than a minute or two. One way or the other, he wouldn't have to tolerate the irritation for long.

The squat, ugly Zula followed Randel into the clearing. He went calmly, eyes clear and steady, ready to accept whatever came his way. In that moment he was a true vampire, nobler than any of the Cubs watching him, and all of them felt humbled.

"What is your choice of weapon?" Zula asked as they squared up to each other.

"Hands are fine by me," Randel said, flexing his fingers.

"As you wish."

Zula lashed out, five sharp nails guaranteed to cut through almost any material on Earth, including the flesh of a vampaneze's throat. But Randel blocked Zula's arm and kicked him in the stomach. Zula grunted and fell back. Randel could have pressed after him, but he held his ground and waited for the vampire to attack again.

Flushed, Zula darted at his foe, then stopped and took a deep breath, regaining his composure. When he was in control of himself, he advanced slowly, studying Randel's eyes for warning signs of what his intentions might be. Larten had thought that Zula was doomed when he accepted the challenge, but watching him now, he believed that maybe the Cub had a chance.

When Zula was within reach, Randel swung a fist at him. Zula blocked it and kicked at Randel's shin. He connected and Randel went down. The vampires roared with excitement, but their cheers were shortlived. As Randel fell, he caught Zula and twisted him around and down. Zula realised too late that his opponent had anticipated his strike. Before he could adjust, he landed heavily on his back — and on the outstretched fingers of one of Randel's hands, which the vampaneze had slyly slid beneath him.

Zula cried out as the vampaneze's nails ripped into his lungs. Then he stiffened, his breath catching in his throat. His legs spasmed, but his arms were strangely still by his sides. He gulped a few times, blood exploding from his mouth, eyes widening, staring at the sun. He had always thought that he would die by the light of the moon. It seemed unfair that a child of the night should perish this way, before the sun had set. He wished Randel had come a few hours later, so he could at least have counted the stars one last time.

And then he wished no more.

Randel shoved the dead vampire away, wiped his hand clean on the grass and stood. He didn't even glance at Zula, but he did cast an eye over the pale-faced vampires sheltering beneath the tree.

"You're a disgrace to your masters," Randel growled, then picked up his cloak, settled it over his head and moved on.

The Cubs stared after the departing vampaneze and watched in silence until he flitted out of sight. Then Larten and Jordan went to fetch the body of Zula Pone. They would burn it later or launch it down a river, depending on what the majority thought the ugly vampire would have preferred.

Tanish was sitting by himself when Larten returned. He had his back to the rest of the Cubs and nobody went near him. They ignored their fallen leader, treating him with the scorn he deserved. Larten felt sorry for his friend, but it couldn't be helped. One of the first things Seba had taught him was that every man made his own decisions in life, and each must stand by the consequences of those choices.

As the sun set, Tanish stood and set off. He didn't say goodbye and nobody asked where he was going. He took nothing, even dropping his expensive coat and discarding his silk shirt. Larten knew, as he watched the disgraced Tanish leave, that this was probably the last they'd see of him. Tanish Eul was no longer part of the clan. He wasn't a traitor, but the Cubs would never mention his name again, and if anyone ever asked about him, they would respond with a simple, damning, "He walks with the humans now."

PART TWO

"If the entire clan stood against her, we would fall."

CHAPTER SIX

The American Civil War was the bloodiest waste of life Larten had yet to witness. Vampires had known about America long before Europeans *discovered* it. One of the clan had sailed with Leif Ericsson and thirty-four others early in the second millennium, and before Paris Skyle became a Prince he stayed Columbus's hand when the human had lost hope and was on the verge of turning back. The elderly vampire would have been saddened to see what had become of the country, but not surprised. Why should these tribes be any different to those they had left behind? People might speak of it being a New World, but they were the same old humans.

Larten watched from a distance as thousands of young men clashed and went to an early grave. He, Wester and Seba had made camp on a hill out of the way of the fighting a few nights earlier. Since then they'd kept vigil, leaving only to hunt and stretch their legs.

The pair of Cubs had abandoned the war packs and returned to their master a few years after Tanish's fall. They had never been able to lose themselves in warfare and other petty pursuits in quite the same way after that dark day. They felt shamed, and the Cubs they cavorted with were a constant reminder of what had happened.

Seba never asked his assistants why they had returned. He was surprised to see them come back to him so early – he hadn't expected them for another decade – but a master didn't need to know everything about his students. He let them keep their secrets and focused on their training.

Seba didn't humiliate them as he had before, or set them tasks they couldn't complete. The pair had changed, Larten in particular, and Seba now deemed them worthy of respect. He believed they were ready to undertake the testing trials that would decide whether or not they were capable of playing an active role in the affairs of the clan.

As Larten studied the warring American factions, he wondered again why Seba had brought them to this place. Their master had never shown an interest in the affairs of humans and hadn't even glanced at the soldiers since they'd arrived. What could have lured him to this maelstrom of slaughter?

Wester stepped up beside the man he thought of as a brother and watched for a while with him. Both were thinking of Tanish Eul.

"How much longer do you think we'll be here?" Wester asked, but Larten only grunted in response. "Did you smell the war pack last night?"

Larten nodded gruffly. "Aye."

Larten's senses had improved greatly in recent years. He'd been aware of the other vampires for the past two nights, but had avoided them, staying by Seba's side, ready to obey his master's orders.

"I miss being part of a pack," Wester sighed. "Feeding on the battlefields was barbaric, but exquisite."

"I am sure reformed opium addicts miss their pipes," Larten said drily. "It does not mean they should return to their old ways."

"It wasn't *that* bad," Wester said.

"No?" Larten shrugged. "I have often told myself that there was nothing wrong in what we did, since so many other vampires were revelling in the bloodshed. But that is no excuse. Humans might not deserve our respect, but they do not merit our contempt either."

Wester smiled. "You sound just like Seba."

Larten winced and scratched his nose, then his ears. He had tried to copy Seba's way of speaking in the past, and Seba had simply corrected him when he made a mistake. But since he'd returned from his time with the Cubs, Seba had taken it more seriously. He had asked Larten if he truly wished to master his vocabulary. When the unsuspecting assistant confirmed that he did, it was the beginning of a new phase, one he had come to despise. He had often begged Seba to stop, but the ancient vampire wouldn't relent.

Under the new regime, when Larten said "don't" or "can't", Seba plucked hairs from his student's nostrils, which was far more painful than Larten would have imagined. After a year of that, he'd tried to outfox his master by burning the hairs from his nose, but Seba set his sights on the hairs in Larten's ears instead and that was even worse! The orange-haired assistant had learnt swiftly in the face of such punishing lessons. He suffered an occasional lapse, but only rarely. It had been weeks since Seba had felt obliged to pluck any hairs.

As Larten and Wester stood watch, Seba joined them and stretched, enjoying the weak evening sun. It had been nearly half a century since he'd met a scared boy in a gloomy crypt and taken him on as an assistant. Seba had aged a lot in that time. His long hair was mostly grey now. He'd shaved his beard and the skin around his throat was dry and wrinkled, covered with old scars and blotches. He looked battered and weary, and groaned if he moved too quickly.

Yet he could set a pace his assistants struggled to match, and he was as light of foot and fast of hand as ever. He often spoke of being near to his end, but Larten suspected his old master might see out this century and perhaps a couple more. Not that he ever said such a thing — he didn't want to invite bad luck.

"Wester thinks I sound like you," Larten said.

"He must be going deaf," Seba huffed. Shading his eyes, he studied the soldiers. They had concluded their killing for the day and were limping back to camp, dragging the wounded, leaving the dead for the creatures of the night which they could sense circling them. "Such noble fools," Seba sighed. "One war should be enough for any race. Why do they go on and on?"

Neither Larten nor Wester tried to answer. They hadn't been vampires anywhere near as long as their master, but as young as they were, both found it hard to recall the time when they had walked as humans, or how their thoughts had functioned in those less blood-riddled days.

"We will move on tonight," Seba said. "Just a few miles. I would be obliged if you carried my coffin."

Larten and Wester fetched Seba's coffin from the rough shelter they had made, then followed him down the hill and around a field of corpses. The younger vampires had not yet developed a taste for coffins. They'd slept in many while travelling with Seba, holed-up in crypts or tombs, but when given a choice they preferred beds. Their master, however, only felt snug with pine walls encaging him and a lid overhead. He had tried several coffins since they'd landed in America. When he finally found one to his liking, he claimed it for his own and begged pardon of the skeleton he'd evicted. His assistants had been carting it around after him ever since.

As the trio followed the course of a small stream, someone called out abruptly from a tree on the other side. "Same old Seba Nile, always has to have the modern conveniences. Can't settle for a stone floor and a roof of sky."

Larten and Wester set the coffin down and squinted. Larten knew the voice, but couldn't place it. As he tried to put a face to it, a shabby vampire dropped from the branches. He was dressed in animal hides and had a couple of belts strapped around his chest, throwing stars hanging loosely from them. He had long green hair. He spat into the stream as he crossed and Larten was fairly sure he heard the General break wind, though it *might* have been the creaking of the trees.

"Vancha March," Seba smiled. "I wondered where the foul stench was coming from."

"I don't know what you're talking about," Vancha scowled. "I bathed last spring, even though I didn't need to." He frowned. "Or was it the spring before?" With a laugh, he tossed a salute to Larten and Wester. "Still hanging around with this old vulture?"

"Someone has to look after him," Larten said.

"He's too weak to carry his own coffin," Wester added.

Larten and Wester hadn't seen the filthy General since their first meeting in Vampire Mountain, so there was much to catch up on. But before they could ask questions, Seba pointed to his coffin and coughed purposefully. Groaning, they picked it up and followed behind at a respectable distance as their master strolled with Vancha and the pair discussed business that was not for the ears of the young.

In time they turned a bend and Larten caught sight of a tent. He might have dismissed it as the camp of a human officer, but Seba and Vancha were heading for it, so he adjusted the coffin on his shoulder and stole a closer look.

The tent was like none he'd seen so far. It was circular, tall and wide, adorned with beautiful, stitched patterns of water flowers and frogs. It looked a bit like the tent in which the Cirque Du Freak performed, but nowhere near the same size. There were three smaller tents around it and a clothesline stood behind them, hung with a variety of dresses and women's undergarments.

A confused Wester nudged Larten, who frowned at the feminine clothes and said, "What sort of a woman would pitch her tent at the edge of a battlefield?"

The answer came to both of them at the same time, but Wester was the one who exclaimed, "A woman of the wilds!"

Sharing a thrilled look, they bustled after their master and his foul-smelling ally, heading for the tent of the woman who – if they had guessed right – was as powerful and as crucial to the fate of the vampire clan as any goddess of legend.

CHAPTER SEVEN

Seba paused at the entrance to the tent and asked Larten and Wester to set aside his coffin. He tugged at his red shirt and cloak, straightened some creases, then examined the material for dirt.

"How do I look?" Vancha asked, spitting into his palm and using it to brush back his green hair.

"Like a cherub," Seba murmured.

"Do you think—"

The flap over the entrance swished back, cutting short his question, and a woman stepped forward. She was short and ugly — she reminded Larten of Zula Pone in some respects — and even filthier than Vancha. She wore no shoes or clothes. Instead there were ropes wrapped around her body. She had pointed ears, a tiny nose, one brown eye and one green. She was as muscular as a man and hairier than most, from a thin beard and moustache down to ten furry toes. Her fingers were stubby and the nails cut short on all of them except the two little fingers, where they grew long and sharp.

Larten thought this was a strange choice of servant for a witch as powerful as the Lady Evanna (if that was indeed who they were coming to meet). He had assumed that Evanna would have pretty, finely dressed maids to wait on her. Maybe she had taken pity on this misfortunate creature and given her a home because nobody else would.

Then, to Larten's astonishment, the short, ugly woman squealed, darted forward and cried, "My little Vancha!" As the General tried to back away in a panic, she hoisted him off the ground and shook him in the air as if he was a large doll.

"Let me down!" Vancha yelled furiously.

"Not until you give me a kiss, you naughty boy," she chortled.

"I'll give you a kick up the—"

"Language, Vancha," she stopped him, squeezing his ribs so hard that his eyes almost popped.

"Apologies... Lady," he wheezed, then pecked her cheek before he suffocated.

The woman smiled and let him drop, then curtsied gracefully to Seba. "You are welcome as always, Master Nile," she said in a soft, melodic voice.

"And grateful for that privilege, my Lady," Seba

said, bowing as he would have before a Prince.

"You've brought a couple of assistants," she noted, turning her brown eye on Larten and her green eye on Wester. Both were gawping at her.

"This is Lar—" Seba began to introduce them.

"I know their names," the woman interrupted. "And I believe they know mine. Don't you, gentlemen?"

"*Evanna?*" Wester gasped, barely able to believe it.

"They expected someone more glamorous," she said to Vancha.

"Many do," he grinned.

"Perhaps this is more what they had in mind." She shimmered and changed shape. She was now tall and lithe, with long blonde hair and an angel's features, clad in a flowing white dress. Larten stared at her, enamoured. He reached out a hand to caress her, then let it drop. He didn't feel he had the right to touch anyone this beautiful.

"Too easily impressed," Evanna tutted, resuming her former appearance. "You shouldn't judge by what's on the outside. Only a fool falls for a pretty face. Are you fools?"

Larten was first to speak this time. "For you, Lady, I would be anything," he said softly, the words springing to his lips.

Evanna raised an eyebrow and glared at him. But as he blinked, confused by her icy look, she realised he

61

wasn't being impudent. "I like this one, Seba," she cooed. "Not the brightest vampire I've ever met, but he has a good heart."

"Both my assistants have good hearts," Seba said. "But is Larten's a heart you might wish to win?"

Evanna laughed at the eagerness of the question. "You're here just a couple of minutes and already you want to pair me off with the nearest vampire to hand." She brushed his cheek fondly and shook her head. "Ask no favours of me yet, old friend. Let us simply enjoy each other's company for a while. I would know all that you have been up to and how things go with the rest of the clan."

Taking his arm, she led the grey-haired vampire inside. After a pause, Larten and Wester followed. Vancha came last, having run another palmful of spit through his hair to make it *extra* stiff and shiny. "If that doesn't impress her," he said smugly to himself, "I don't know what will!"

Evanna was Desmond Tiny's daughter. He had created her a thousand years ago, mixing the blood of a vampire with that of a pregnant wolf. She was a powerful enchantress who could work many magical charms. But the night-walkers were most interested in one particular ability of hers.

Vampires couldn't have children. That was the way it had always been. To keep the race alive, they needed to blood humans. The clan used to think that would always be the case, but Evanna had the power to bear a vampire's child. If she chose, she could breed with a vampire and her offspring would be able to reproduce too.

Vampires had been wooing Evanna for hundreds of years. Mr Tiny had warned that she and her young would have the power to wipe out the clan, but they cared nothing about the risks. The possibility of being able to rear children of their own was intoxicating.

But Evanna had so far shunned their advances. She had never taken a vampire as a mate, or given any hint that she intended to. Still they sought her out and tried to win her heart, fighting in her name, offering her gifts, doing all that they could to make her theirs. To no avail.

Larten secretly hoped to captivate the legendary Lady of the Wilds. He had a way with ladies – few had been able to resist his charms when he was a Cub – and he was confident that she would fall for him as many others had. If Evanna mated with him, he'd become the founding father of a new generation of vampires and his power and fame would be assured.

"I would have worn finer clothes if I had known we

were coming here," he whispered to Wester as they sat on a couch laden with feather pillows.

"Don't worry," Wester grinned. "If Vancha is your only opposition, you can't fail."

Though Wester had also dreamt of winning the hand of the famed Lady, now that he'd seen the intent in Larten's eyes, he put such thoughts from his mind. He always gave way to his best friend. They had never fought over a woman or anything else that Larten set his sights on. Wester thought of Lartèn as his brother and he loved the orange-haired vampire totally. He never tried to take the things which Larten desired, even if he craved them himself.

The tent seemed larger inside than out. There was a plush bed in the centre, paintings hanging from beams, statues set around the sides. Huge candles burnt steadily, while bowls and jugs overflowed with fruit, vegetables, water and wine. There was no meat or fish, which surprised Larten until he recalled a rumour that Evanna didn't eat anything that couldn't be grown.

Three young women brought the bowls and jugs to the vampires once they were seated. All were dressed in plain white shirts and beige trousers. Larten had only rarely seen a woman in trousers and his gaze kept flicking over the servants. One of them – she had long dark hair and sharp grey eyes – caught him looking and glared challengingly. He tried his infamous smile on her – it set most women's legs wobbling – but her glare only deepened. Surprised and unsettled, Larten coughed and turned his head aside. Wester saw this and hid a smile.

"First things first," Evanna said, lying on a *chaise longue* and plucking a grape from a tray. "How has my little Vancha been? Tell mommy all."

"*Mommy?*" Larten gasped.

"I wish you wouldn't say things like that," Vancha grimaced. "I don't call you a witch, do I?"

"With good reason," Evanna snapped, eyes flashing. "I'll cut out the tongue of anyone who calls me that. I'm the world's most powerful sorceress, a priestess of dark arts, mother of the future and Lady of the Wilds. You, on the other hand, will always be my sweet, cuddly Vancha. I still remember feeding you and the way you used to burp when you were done." She giggled. "That much hasn't changed."

"Evanna found me when I was a baby," Vancha muttered to Larten and Wester. "My parents had been killed and I'd been left to die. She rescued me and carried me with her for a few years before handing me over to... someone else," he finished vaguely.

Evanna's smile faded. "You make it sound as if I carried you alone," she said softly.

"As *I* remember it, Lady, you did," Vancha said, and there was an edge to his tone now which surprised the younger pair of vampires.

Evanna held Vancha's gaze for a few seconds, then shook her head and sighed. "A man should never turn his back on his—"

"Please!" Vancha snapped. "Let the past lie."

"The past never lies buried forever," Evanna muttered. "We cannot hide from those to whom we are bound by nature. But if you wish to keep your silly secrets, so be it. You know that I only ever wished the best for you."

"And I'm grateful to you for that," Vancha said, his features softening. Then he spat and winked. "I just wish you didn't treat me like a damn child."

Evanna laughed. "When you have a few more centuries under your belt, I will consider you an adult. Until then…" She pinched his cheek.

"Charna's guts!" Vancha roared. "You go too far!" He threw himself at her and they rolled across the floor of the tent. He was punching and kicking at the witch, but she only laughed and tossed him clear. As he landed, he whipped a star from his belt and launched it at her head.

Evanna plucked the deadly throwing star from the air and calmly picked her teeth with one of the prongs.

"Still playing with your shurikens?" she mumbled. "I thought you would have found a new toy by now."

Vancha looked like he would attack again, but in the end he threw back his head and laughed. "By the gods of the vampires, you're a piece of work! Come, let's drink toasts to absent friends and sing songs of the old nights."

"I will drink with you any time, my dear," Evanna said. "And with your companions too." She clicked her fingers at the servants. "Milk for Master March." Then she looked at the others. "Ale, I suppose?"

"Aye!" Larten and Wester exclaimed.

"Why not?" Seba added with a smile.

Barrels of the finest ale Larten had ever tasted were brought, and the rest of the night was a blur for him from that moment on.

CHAPTER EIGHT

Larten woke in the afternoon with a pounding head. He was in a hammock, though he had no recollection of getting into it. As he rose, he saw that someone had painted a series of tattoos on his hand with a piece of charcoal or some similar marker. He frowned, thought about making investigations, then decided he was better not knowing. Groaning, he made his way to a barrel of rainwater outside and dunked his head.

When he came up for air, one of Evanna's assistants – the one with the dark hair and grey eyes – was standing beside him, holding out a mug of something hot and steaming.

"Drink this," she said.

"It's not ale, is it?" Larten asked, face whitening at the thought.

The assistant smiled briefly – she looked quite pretty when she smiled – then shook her head. "A cure of my mistress's. You will feel better after you drink it."

Larten had tried a number of hangover cures in the past, none of which had done much for him. But to be polite he took the mug from the woman – not much more than a girl when seen by daylight – and downed half of it. He finished off the rest a few moments later and almost immediately his headache began to lift.

"This is amazing," he gasped. "What is in it?"

"You'd feel sick again if I told you," the girl laughed. She had crooked teeth, Larten noted, but a man could easily ignore a flaw like that.

"I do not think you told me your name," Larten said smoothly.

"You think wrong," she answered. "In fact you made up a song about it. *Lovely Arra Sails, nectar to all males, how I'd like to spear you like a whaler spears a whale!* There was more, but that, sadly, was the best line."

Larten winced. "I have a habit of making up insulting rhymes when drunk. My apologies."

"No need. Your songs about my two sisters were worse. But they were nearly as drunk as you, so I doubt they'll remember."

"Three sisters working for the same mistress? That is unusual."

"They're not my real sisters," Arra sighed, as if explaining something obvious to an idiot. "That's just how Evanna refers to us." She shrugged. "They're pleasant enough, though I don't think of them as friends." Arra squinted at Larten and pursed her lips. "You're a vampire, aren't you?"

"Aye," Larten said proudly.

"Don't vampires perish in direct sunlight?"

"Not immediately. I would start to burn if I stayed out, but it would not kill me for a couple of hours. A lot of the myths are false or distortions of the truth."

"Evanna doesn't talk much about vampires, except to complain about how you follow her around like dogs."

Larten scowled at that, but said nothing. He headed back inside, but Arra blocked his way. "That's my tent over there." She nodded at one of the three small tents that stood next to Evanna's. "If you have no pressing business, I'd like to talk with you and learn more about vampires."

Larten arched a merry eyebrow.

"When I say talk, I *mean* talk," Arra growled, reading his mind. "You tried to kiss me last night."

"How did you respond?" Larten asked.

Arra smiled. "Let's just say the next verse of your song began with, *Nasty Arra Sails, she has a vicious tongue.*"

Larten managed a laugh, then followed Arra into her tent. Like Evanna's, it was larger than it looked from the outside, though it was plainly decorated and

Arra didn't have many personal belongings. The pair sat on her bed – Arra making sure there was a discreet distance between them – and Larten spoke for a long time about his life, the clan and Vampire Mountain. Arra listened with silent interest to everything. It was only when he spoke about flitting that she interrupted.

"My mistress can flit too. And she can breathe out a gas to make people faint, although she rarely needs to. Do you think the vampires inherited their magic from Evanna or her father?"

"Have you met Desmond Tiny?" Larten asked.

"No. But I have heard of him through visitors like yourself."

Larten had always taken the magical talents of the clan for granted, such as their longevity, strength and speed. But now that he thought about it, he realised that such gifts were mysterious. Had their supernatural talents developed naturally, or were they the work of a meddler with more power? Larten made a mental note to ask Seba later, though he had a feeling his master wouldn't be able to answer the question either.

"Tell me about yourself," Larten said, changing the subject. "How did you come to work for Evanna? Are you the age you look or are you old like your mistress?"

"*Old?*" Arra screeched, chucking a pillow at him.

"Manners, vampire, or I'll stake you to the ground outside and leave you to burn."

As Larten smiled, she relaxed and told him a bit about where she'd come from, how she'd run away from home in search of adventure and found Evanna. "Or was found by her," Arra added suspiciously. "I've a feeling she sends for apprentices. We don't just wander into her life, even if we seem to."

Evanna had taught Arra a few spells, but mostly the girl was employed as a servant, to cater to her mistress's guests and clean up after them. She wasn't happy about that. She wanted to learn the secrets of Evanna's world and become a mighty sorceress.

"It's not as if she even needs us," Arra complained. "I've seen her snap her fingers and conjure up a full meal, or wave a hand at a dirty room and suddenly it's clean. She just likes having servants to boss around."

"Why don't you leave?" Larten asked.

"I will," Arra said. "But I don't want to move on until I have somewhere else to go. I fled without direction once, when I left home, but I'd rather not leave everything to chance a second time."

Her eyes narrowed. She started to ask Larten something, but then somebody whistled in the distance and she grimaced. "My mistress wants me."

"She whistles for you like a dog?" Larten grinned.

"If you laugh, I'll poison your next drink," Arra growled, then hurried to see what Evanna wanted. Larten followed, still smiling. It had been nice, chatting with Arra. She was a sharp little thing, and scowls came easier to her than smiles, but Larten liked her. He hoped they could be friends, at least for a while, before he moved on with Seba and Wester. After that he figured it was unlikely that he would ever see the surly-looking girl again.

CHAPTER NINE

They spent two more nights with the Lady of the Wilds. Other vampires came to see her while they were present. Most were from the war pack shadowing the warring humans, but some had come from further away, crossing oceans as Seba and his assistants had.

A few of the Cubs recognised Larten and Wester, and greeted Larten by his nickname. It had been some years since he'd been called Quicksilver and he found it oddly unsettling. That part of his life was behind him and he wished to move on. Though he was polite to the Cubs who had once been his friends, he made no effort to renew any of those friendships.

Evanna hosted most of her visitors openly, but sometimes she sent Seba and his assistants away so that she could greet a newcomer in private. She seemed to know what each of her guests would prefer, and did what she could to satisfy their requirements — except agree to their pleas to accept them as her partner.

"We came to this country just to meet Evanna, didn't we?" Wester asked Seba on the third night as they were resting on a nearby hill after they had slipped into one of the soldiers' camps to feed.

Seba nodded. "You are as sharp as ever, Master Flack. Evanna would rather the clan left her alone. She tires of our endless proposals. But she knows how highly we regard her, so she sets aside several nights every now and then for us to court her. A favoured few are welcome at her home too, but most have to settle for meetings like this."

"Where does she live?" Wester asked.

Seba shook his head. "If she wants you to know, she will tell you."

"So you brought us here for her to have a look at us, in case she liked our faces?" Larten asked.

"Aye." Seba rubbed the back of his neck and sighed. "We believe Evanna will choose a mate one night, either a vampire or a vampaneze, but—"

"A vampaneze?" Wester barked. "She consorts with them too?"

"She meets with all creatures of the night," Seba said calmly. "Evanna makes no distinction between us. The vampaneze are as dear to her as we are. She tries to keep us apart — she will move to a new site soon, I think, where she will meet with our blood cousins —

but if a vampaneze came here we would have to treat him with respect."

"I wouldn't," Wester snarled. "If I spot any of those scum, I'll—"

"—do nothing but bid him a good night," Seba said bluntly and there was an edge to his voice that his assistants rarely heard. "If you anger Evanna, she will crush you. Never let her charm blind you to the fact that she is Desmond Tiny's daughter. Respect her wishes when in her presence, Wester, or no words of mine will be enough to save you."

Wester glowered at his master. To ease the tension, Larten asked how Seba had known that Evanna would be here.

"She led me here," Seba answered vaguely. "Those who seek Evanna simply follow their feet. I did not know this was where we would end up when we set out. All I knew was that we would find her wherever she wanted to be found."

"And you really hoped that one of us would seduce her?" Larten pressed.

Seba chuckled. "I doubt if anyone will ever *seduce* Evanna. But you made a good attempt, Larten. I did not know you were so smooth with the ladies."

"I am usually more successful," Larten grunted sourly. All of his flattering words, sideways looks and tricks had fallen flat on the witch. She had been kind to him and laughed at his jokes, but never given the least hint that she might consider him as a mate.

"Do not be too hard on yourself," Seba said. "Many fine vampires have been rejected before you, and many will be in the future too, I am sure. As I was about to say before Wester interrupted, we believe she will choose a mate eventually, but we do not know which qualities she is looking for, or even if she *is* looking — maybe she is waiting for a certain time or event.

"Since we know so little of her heart, many of us come to see her from time to time, and bring our assistants when they are ready for such a meeting. We continue to hope that one night she will claim one of us as her own. But so far, no luck."

"What if she takes a vampaneze?" Wester growled.

"We fear that more than anything," Seba said. "Evanna has the power to destroy the clan. If she chooses to mate with a vampaneze, their children will certainly gain some of her magical powers. Maybe the dreaded Lord of the Vampaneze will be a child of Evanna's."

"Then why don't we strike?" Wester hissed. "Kill her or abduct her and make her do as we wish?"

"If this foolishness continues, I will whip you until

the flesh of your back peels from your spine like a snake's shedded skin," Seba rumbled.

Wester blinked with shock. The old vampire had never threatened either of them like this before. There had been many cuffs and kicks over the years, but never a savage, brutal vow.

Seba saw the hurt in his assistant's eyes and softened. "Understand me," he said gently. "She is much stronger than any of us — than *all* of us. If the entire clan stood against her, we would fall."

"Surely no one is that powerful," Larten said dubiously.

"I do not exaggerate," Seba insisted. "Her power is not of this world. There are myths of gods raising countries, levelling mountains, making the seas churn. I do not know if those stories are true, but I believe Evanna could do all that and more. So let me never hear either of you plotting against her. She would be an enemy far greater than any other, with the exception of her meddling father."

Seba looked into the eyes of his assistants, trying to make sure his words had sunk home. He saw that he had made an impact and hoped it would be enough to prevent future follies.

"Now," he said, forcing a smile. "Let us return and say nothing more about this. Only, if she *should* at any time bat her eyelids at you, do not bother with a long courtship!"

Larten and Wester laughed weakly, then trailed Seba back to the tent, all three silent and immersed in thought.

The tent had been dismantled when they returned. Evanna's apprentices were standing behind a cart, glumly preparing to push. There was no way everything from inside the tent could fit on to the cart – the canvas itself would have required a wagon – but Larten wasn't surprised. The Lady of the Wilds could work many wonders.

"Time to be off," Evanna said cheerfully. "I've had fewer visitors than normal. The clan must be losing interest in me."

"Have you far to travel, Lady?" Seba asked, kissing her cheeks.

"You know very well that I go to greet my other admirers nearby," Evanna said.

Seba smiled. "Aye, but I would rather not admit it."

"Foolish children," Evanna snapped. "Why don't you put your squabbles behind you and reunite? Life would be much easier if you did."

"It is not that simple," Seba sighed. "We are bound by strings of destiny."

"We're all bound by those," Evanna said hollowly, a sad look crossing her face. Then she shook her head and picked up Vancha, who had stayed behind while the others hunted. "Farewell, my little baby."

"Let me go!" he roared, clubbing her ears.

She laughed and kissed his nose. As he struggled and swore, she kissed his lips. His arms and legs relaxed and he was smiling shyly when she set him down again. Evanna turned to Wester and Larten. The witch was no fairer than she had been when he first saw her, but Larten no longer noticed her ugliness.

"It was a pleasure to meet you," she said.

"It was our honour, my Lady," Wester replied, bowing.

"An honour," Larten echoed, then knelt on one knee and took her dirty hand. "I would like to visit you again sometime, if you can find it in your heart to grant me permission."

"He's bold, this one," Evanna chuckled. She slipped her hand out of Larten's and gripped his chin. Tilting his head back, she gazed down at him. He thought for a moment that her eyes had traded places – hadn't the blue one been on the right before? – but then she spoke and he lost interest in such trivialities.

"My home is my refuge from the world. I invite only a select handful of my closest friends to visit me there. Why should I welcome a snip of a vampire like you?"

He had the feeling that if he gave the wrong answer, he would never see the Lady of the Wilds again. Trying not to worry about that, he grinned shakily and said, "I am good with a flannel. If you ever cared to take a bath, I could scrub your back."

Evanna blinked slowly. Larten could see her pondering whether to laugh or rip his head off. Fortunately for the young vampire, she chose to see the funny side of his proposition.

"Bold as a monkey," Evanna chortled, releasing Larten's chin and thumbing his nose. "A strange choice of assistant, Seba, but I like him. Aye, Larten Crepsley, you may visit any time the fancy takes you." She pressed a finger to his forehead and he felt something buzz deep inside his brain. "You will be able to find me whenever you wish."

Evanna nodded at Wester politely, and although he couldn't suppress a stab of jealousy, he managed a genuine smile. This confirmed what he had always thought — Larten was in some way superior to him, destined for greater things. Wester would have liked to be a vampire of import, but the world needed its secondary players too. There was no point wishing he could be more than he was. He was happy to make the most of whatever life had set aside for him.

Then the witch was off, slouching away, looking like a crazy woman who had escaped from bedlam. Arra Sails and the other apprentices shuffled after her, groaning as they pushed the cart. Arra rolled her eyes at Larten and he smiled sympathetically.

"Very well, gentlemen," Seba exclaimed before the women had moved out of sight. "We have wasted enough years. It is time to return to more pressing matters. Grab your belongings and prepare for a hard trek. We make for Vampire Mountain immediately."

PART THREE

"It means respect."

CHAPTER TEN

It was time for another Council at Vampire Mountain. Vampires travelled from all over the world to meet old friends, challenge one another, debate laws, tell tall tales and have a grand time. Larten and Wester were kept busy in advance, helping out in the gaming halls, preparing the rooms for the chaos of the Festival of the Undead.

The pair had been permanent fixtures in the mountain for the past few years. Both had passed their Trials of Initiation – five perilous tasks which all vampires had to overcome – not long after they'd returned with Seba. Larten took his Trials several months before Wester and sailed through, but Wester almost failed. In his second Trial he'd faced two wild boars that had been driven insane with vampire blood. He managed to kill them, but one speared him with its tusks before it died and he had struggled to complete his last three Trials.

Seba had visited Wester before his third Trial and asked if he'd made peace with the vampire gods. Death was nothing to be afraid of as long as one was ready for it. Wester had nodded soberly and said he could die with no regrets if that was his fate.

Wester had summoned Larten a while later and told him what their master had said. Then, in a soft voice, he'd said, "I lied. I want you to make me a promise. It's a lot to ask, and I'll understand if you refuse, but if I die, I want you to track down and kill Murlough for me."

Larten had almost made the promise — even though the vampaneze had spared their lives when they were his to take — but something in Wester's expression stopped him. The Trials of Initiation were as much a mental as a physical obstacle. If you lost belief in yourself, it could prove as fatal as losing an arm or leg.

"Murlough is your nemesis, not mine," Larten had said icily. "If you die, I will not pursue him on your behalf. I would not ask you to take my enemies as your own, and you should not ask it of me."

Wester had been surprised and hurt, but he'd accepted Larten's decision and grimly battled through the rest of his Trials, spurred on by his desire to survive and gain revenge for the slaughter of his family.

The pair had been studying hard under Seba and others since then, taking the first steps on the long road to becoming vampire Generals. Much of their time was spent learning the intricacies of combat. They would often pass entire nights in a gaming Hall, sparring with each other, overseen by a tutor.

One of their tutors now bellowed at them to empty a chest full of axes. "What are you waiting for? The last vampire arrived three hours ago. The Festival starts at sunset. Perhaps you want them to hunt for the axes, to make a game of it?"

"Sorry, Vanez!" they roared, speeding up even though they had been working fast already.

Vanez Blane glared at the assistants, then moved on. He was in a foul mood. This was his first time working in the gaming Halls ahead of Council. The guards normally took care of such matters, but they'd been understaffed this year and he had volunteered to help. He regretted his offer now. So much to think about and take care of. He was determined not to fall into this trap again. As soon as Council finished he'd be off, and he would make sure he never got caught for duty like this a second time. He belonged in the wilds, not cooped up inside a mountain!

As busy and stressed as he was, Larten was looking forward to Council. The last few years had been dull and strenuous. While he didn't regret his choice to join Seba again and devote himself to his studies, he missed the outside world, the travel, nights spent drinking, gambling and flattering ladies, the thrill of warfare.

Larten was pleased with how he was developing. He learnt swiftly and improved quickly. He wasn't the biggest of vampires, but his speed and skills helped him get the better of most opponents. The nights of Larten being a punching bag for others were long gone.

Yet he wasn't truly happy. He couldn't put his finger on the reason for his discontent. He just felt as if he'd come here before he was finished with the world. He had no desire to be a Cub again or to run with a war pack, but he felt like he was missing out on *something*.

He often thought about Vur Horston and the plans they had made as children to explore every last inch of the world. Even though Larten had travelled the globe widely, he wanted to see more of it, to honour the memory of his lost cousin. Of course he would be able to do that once he became a General – he could spend the rest of his life roaming if he wished – but Larten was impatient. He wanted to do it all and see it all *now*.

Still, he wouldn't have to endure life inside the mountain much longer. Every vampire was forced to undergo a degree of training here if they wished to become a General, but the majority of their lessons could be learnt on the road. Seba would take Larten and Wester away from here soon, perhaps at the end of Council, and they could study at a more relaxed pace while travelling far and wide as they had in the past.

When they'd finished setting out the axes, Larten and Wester reported to Vanez for further instructions. He kept them darting around the Halls and tunnels for the next few hours, yelling at them even when they worked speedily and efficiently. Larten was on the point of snapping back when Vanez suddenly smiled at the pair.

"You've done well," he said. "Go get ready for the Festival. And please forgive me if I vented my frustrations on you."

"Nothing to forgive," Larten grinned, then shared an excited look with Wester. They hurried down to the Hall of Perta Vin-Grahl for a quick wash, then to the cave they shared with Seba and five others, to pull on their finest clothes and make sure they looked their best for the opening ceremony.

* * *

The first few hours of the Festival were crazy as usual, vampires fighting as if the clan was on the point of extinction and there would be nobody left for them to battle the following night. Bones were shattered, limbs were severed and four vampires made a premature journey to Paradise, their friends cheering them on — dying in combat was a noble way to perish.

Larten let himself be washed along with the tide of warring vampires – there was no point trying to fight it – but as soon as things calmed down a little he went in search of a particular opponent. He didn't know the vampire's name, only that he was tall and burly, with a nose that had been broken many times. The General had mocked Larten when easily defeating him in a challenge the first time he'd come to Council. Larten had been looking forward to facing him again ever since.

Larten was challenged a few times while searching for the General and he had to respond to each – you weren't supposed to avoid a contest during the Festival – but finally he found his man standing by the bars in the Hall of Oceen Pird, watching two vampires with round-ended staffs trying to knock each other flying.

"You!" Larten shouted, pounding the vampire's back.

The General looked around and scowled. He didn't remember this young pup, but something about the orange hair struck a chord.

"Wrestle with me," Larten growled.

The vampire smiled bitterly and turned. Larten's heart sank — the General's right arm was missing from just beneath the shoulder.

"Why the long face?" the General snapped, then glanced at the space where his arm should be. "Surely *this* won't deter you? It's just a flesh wound."

"I..." Larten hesitated.

"... don't want to fight a cripple?" the General asked softly, fire burning in his eyes.

Larten stiffened. "I have no intention of offending you with pity. I was merely going to say that I did not want to have an unfair advantage. So..." He pulled his right arm inside his shirt, tucking it in tight.

The General gawped at Larten, then laughed. "That's a first! Have at me, then, youngster, and may the luck of the vampires be with you."

Larten moved in on the General and tried to get a grip with his left arm. But he wasn't used to fighting one-handed. The General, who'd had years to adapt, threw the younger vampire to the floor and pinned him with his legs.

"One to me," he grinned as Larten rose and dusted

himself off, then went on to throw his challenger two more times in quick succession.

Larten hadn't imagined the fight going this way, but then again he'd planned to use both arms. As he picked himself up for a third time, all he could do was laugh at the unexpected direction which the bout had taken.

Many years ago the General had mocked Larten and walked off contemptuously after defeating him. But this time he helped the orange-haired vampire to his feet and embraced him warmly.

"I might have beaten you with ease, but you've earned my respect, young one. It's not easy fighting one-handed. You didn't have to challenge me on my own terms. By doing so, you proved you have courage and dignity, as well as something even more elusive — style! We'll fight again sometime, when you've had more practice with a single arm, aye?"

"Aye," Larten chuckled.

They drank much and spoke of many things that night. The General told Larten about some of the times his nose had been broken and the great vampires he had faced in challenges over the years. But he never mentioned his name, or if he did, Larten failed to note it.

Over the coming years Larten often trained with an arm tied behind his back. But he never got to test himself against the broken-nosed General again, for he died soon after Council in a fight with a panther. He was alone and his passage went unmarked, but if anyone had been present, they would have seen him smile just before his throat was ripped open. They wouldn't have known what he was grinning about, but he was fondly remembering the night when a young, orange-haired assistant had challenged him to a one-armed wrestling match in the Hall of Oceen Pird.

CHAPTER ELEVEN

Night gave way to day and most of the vampires went to rest for a few hours or tend to their injuries. At sunset they gathered in the huge Hall of Stahrvos Glen for the traditional howling contest. At the signal, every vampire howled loudly and tried to sustain it. The one who held his howl the longest would be afforded the title "of the Howl" for the next twelve years.

Larten didn't have a particularly impressive howl and he faded from the contest early. But two vampires he knew well were among the last three. One was his old Cub ally, Yebba, who seemed to have grown even larger since Larten last saw him. The other was a less familiar acquaintance, Mika Ver Leth.

Larten was surprised to see Mika – dressed in black as always – among the final trio. Normally the successful howlers were bulky and large-lunged, like Yebba, but Mika was of average height and slender. Yet he was holding his own against the others. Larten cheered on Yebba because of their friendship, but secretly he hoped Mika would take the honours — he had always had a soft spot for an underdog.

Yebba came to a sudden, choking stop and scowled, disgusted with himself. Mika and the other General carried on for another minute, the chords in their throats strained to breaking point, tears coursing from their eyes. Mika was in trouble – his voice was wavering – but then the other vampire fainted without warning and it was over.

A huge cheer went up and Mika was engulfed by Generals eager to toast his name and be the first to challenge him to a fight. Larten bumped into him later that night and hailed him as Mika of the Howl.

"It sounds strange," Mika said, managing a rare, thin smile.

"Were you surprised to win?" Larten asked.

"No," Mika said. "I practised for the last decade. I took singing lessons from a human tenor and he taught me how to extend a note."

Larten frowned. "Why? It surely cannot mean that much to you."

"It means respect," Mika said seriously. "I hope to be a Prince one night and I want to be invested sooner rather than later. As trivial as this contest was, it got me noticed and that's important."

Larten was amused by the ambitious General. Most vampires weren't political — they didn't care about power games and moving up the ranks. Mika was more like a human in that respect. But the clan was changing. The world was becoming hostile as mankind bred in ever greater numbers and claimed more territory. Vampires would have to keep an even lower profile than before if they were to survive. That meant taking the clan in a new direction. They would need youthful, imaginative leaders. A hundred years ago Mika wouldn't have got far in his quest to be a Prince, but Larten believed he might prosper in the current climate. He wished Mika luck in his princely pursuit, even though it wasn't a goal he personally aspired to.

But Mika wasn't the only one earning respect at that Council. Although he was unaware of it, Larten had caught the eye of many of his peers and was beginning to make a name for himself. The clan approved of the way he had faced the one-armed General, and although he'd lost that challenge, he had won most of his subsequent contests, defeating a host of older, more experienced vampires.

Paris Skyle heard of the youngster's success and sought out his friend Seba to congratulate him.

"The credit is not mine," Seba said with a smile,

watching from the sides as Wester struggled with a vampire who had only been blooded within the last couple of years. "Larten is driven by an inner passion. I have helped him, I hope, but he cannot be moulded, merely guided."

"He could go far, according to the rumours," Paris murmured.

Seba sighed. "Is that so important? If he lives a good life and is true to himself, should that not be enough?"

"My words stung you," Paris said, surprised. "Forgive me."

"You do not need to apologise, Sire," Seba said. "I have heard others talk highly of Larten, but they have noticed no merits which I had not already seen many years ago, even when I first met him as a child. I have always known that he will climb high, if he chooses to climb."

Paris frowned. "You hope that he won't."

Seba pulled a face. "Larten could be a great General, maybe even a Prince. I will be delighted if that is his aim and he achieves it. But I will be just as pleased if he merely wants to lead a clean, honest life. I have no desire to be a mentor of Princes. I simply hope that those I care about are content."

"Do you worry about what power will do to him?" Paris asked, recalling a time when he had offered Seba the chance to become a Prince. "Do you think he is not suited to a position of authority?"

Seba shrugged. "Think it? No. *Fear* it? Aye. Whether my fears are well-founded or not, I cannot say. He is much like I was at that age. Perhaps I see flaws which are not there, reflections of my own weaknesses. Only time will tell. Either way, there is no point worrying about the future. He could break his back tonight and that would be the end of the matter."

"The gods give and the gods take away," Paris agreed.

Across from them, Wester finally got the better of his opponent and the pair went to drink each other's health. Wester was beaming — he didn't enjoy many victories. Seba was pleased for him. He worried about Wester too, but felt his weaker assistant might find his path sooner than Larten, and take to it with more ease. He suspected Larten didn't yet understand his true desires, and there was nothing harder than chasing a dream if you didn't know what it was.

As if reading his friend's thoughts, Paris said, "Have you told them your good news?"

"No. I will wait until after the Ceremony of Conclusion."

"Do you think that they will stay with you?"

"Wester, aye. Larten... I do not know." Quietly he added, "I hope not."

"Come!" Paris boomed, taking his friend's arm. "I've darkened your mood. Let me lighten it again with a glass of wine."

"Wine?" Seba smiled. "I thought we only drank ale at Council."

Paris winked. "Ale is fine for younger, less sophisticated palates, but it's the juice of the grape for veterans like us, aye?"

"Aye," Seba chuckled and went to try and drown his worries with the Prince.

The children of the clan began departing Vampire Mountain a few nights after the Ceremony of Conclusion, once their heads had cleared and they could stand without wobbling. It was an undramatic exodus. Most didn't even bother to bid their friends farewell, especially the older vampires, since that wasn't their custom. They simply slipped away, some heading off in specific directions, others wandering wherever their feet took them.

Larten and Wester helped clear up inside the Halls and tunnels. It was a mammoth task, even more involved than the preparations beforehand. But it was a calmer time and they went about their work in a merry mood. Even Vanez Blane was relaxed now, often stopping to joke with the pair and tell them not to work too hard. He had already forgotten the stressful lead-up to Council and was thinking about offering his services again in the future.

Seba let the dust settle before summoning his assistants to a meeting in the Hall of Khledon Lurt. Over a bowl of bat broth, he told them of his exciting offer.

"The Princes have asked me to become the quartermaster of Vampire Mountain. I have accepted."

Wester had expected the announcement — he had heard rumours during the Festival — but Larten was taken by complete surprise.

"Quartermaster?" he frowned, pushing his bowl aside. "I thought you did not yearn for power."

"I do not want to become a Prince," Seba corrected him. "Quartermaster is a very different proposition. I will wield no actual authority. In theory I will be responsible only for taking care of supplies and keeping the Halls tidy. But as you know, in reality the quartermaster has a huge say on everything that happens in Vampire Mountain, not just at Council but the rest of the time. Princes and Generals come and go as needs dictate, but the quartermaster is ever present. I will have the task of approving tutors and guards, determining how and what students are taught. I will have the ears of the Princes — the *ear* in

Paris Skyle's case – and they will listen carefully to my opinions."

"They do that anyway," Larten said.

"Perhaps," Seba smiled. "But it is a different situation now. I cannot command as I could if I became a Prince. But if I live a long time – and the gods seem unwilling to take my soul, even though I am old and weary – I will be able to exert a strong influence for many decades to come. I can be a link between the old ways and the new. I think the clan needs someone like that right now."

Seba studied his assistants, awaiting their reaction. As he had suspected, Wester responded enthusiastically. "Congratulations, master. You deserve this and I know you'll be a credit to the clan."

Larten wasn't sure what to say. He already had an idea what this would mean for him and he was struggling with which path to take now that he had come to an unexpected fork in the road.

"Aye," Larten muttered. "Congratulations. May the luck of the vampires be with you."

Seba nodded, then said as lightly as he could, "What will the pair of you do now? I do not expect you to stay. I imagine you will want to leave and—"

"No!" Wester exclaimed. "I'll stay. I still have much to learn and nobody can teach me better than you."

"Are you certain?" Seba asked, ignoring the flattery. "It will be twenty or thirty years before you can become a General. That is a long time for a young vampire to spend caged inside a mountain."

"I don't care," Wester said stubbornly. "I'm staying. You will too, won't you, Larten?" There was a faint, desperate edge to Wester's voice. He was trying to sound casual, but he knew Larten was eager to leave. He didn't want to be forced to choose between his best friend and his mentor.

Larten didn't reply immediately. His brow furrowed as he considered his options. Seba longed to advise Larten to leave, but thought it would be wrong of him to try and influence his uncertain assistant, so he held his tongue.

"Stay," Wester hissed. "This place isn't so bad. You'd have to look for a new master if you left."

"There are many who would accept you," Seba murmured, interceding only to counter the pressure that Wester was exerting. "You made a fine impression at Council and would have your choice of tutors, perhaps even Paris Skyle or another Prince."

Larten's eyes narrowed. The Princes trained only those with great potential, the vampires who might become powerful Generals and replace them further down the line. This was the first indication he'd had that the path to the Hall of Princes might open up to him in the future. Mika Ver Leth would have jumped at such an opportunity, but Larten wasn't Mika and he didn't hunger for power. Yet it was tempting...

Larten glanced at Wester and saw both hope and fear in his blood-brother's eyes. It was ridiculous. The pair were in their sixties. They would have been great-grandfathers with at least one foot in the grave if they hadn't been blooded. Men of their age should have long outgrown the need for a best friend.

But they were young as vampires measured such things, and hadn't been apart since facing Murlough in the ruins of the old house. The pair had gone through much together, blooding, training, running with war packs. Larten would be lonely if they parted, but it would be harder on Wester. In the long run it might be better for him — Wester thought of himself too much as a lesser brother and maybe he needed some time apart from Larten to grow. But in the short term it would hurt.

Larten tried to distance himself from Wester's feelings, to decide what *he* wanted. But it was difficult. He felt – wrongly – that Seba would be disappointed if he left. The old vampire might think that Larten hoped to learn more from another master. He should have known better – Seba had made it clear on many occasions that the time would come when his assistants would need to establish their own lives — but his thoughts were jumbled up.

Finally Larten sighed and went with the easiest option. "I will stay," he said glumly.

Wester cheered and hugged him. Seba smiled, but inside he was troubled. When he retired to his coffin the following morning he lay awake for a long time, plagued by an uneasy feeling, wondering if he should have spoken up rather than let Larten make what he believed to be a potentially damaging call.

CHAPTER TWELVE

The next few years were difficult for Larten. Training to be a General was a hard time for any vampire. To start with, he had to master a variety of weapons, even though he would never use most of them. Larten looked forward to his knife and axe lessons, but there were others – like the throwing stars Vancha favoured, and a spiked, four-headed club – which he loathed. There was no such thing as an easy lesson. He was thrown in at the deep end every time and forced to defend himself in the face of a very real attack by his tutor. Larten spent many weeks nursing broken bones, and was concussed so often that he regularly couldn't get to sleep because of the ringing in his ears.

What particularly depressed him was that Wester was making relatively smooth progress. His younger friend suffered a vast array of injuries, the same as every trainee, but nowhere near anything like Larten's. And it didn't seem to matter how hard the orange-haired assistant worked — he always came to more grief in his lessons than Wester or the others in their group.

What Larten didn't know was that his tutors were working him harder than the rest. It wasn't a conspiracy, simply the way they operated. When the taskmasters of Vampire Mountain trained someone with above average ability, they set him especially gruelling tasks. Vampires were ruthless. They had no time for weakness and weeded out those who would be of no benefit to the clan. This was widely known. But many of the trainees were unaware that their masters were as harsh with those who had the potential to become leaders. If a tutor thought a student had talent, he pushed the youth to his limit, to either exploit or exhaust his potential. If Larten stayed the course and proved himself worthy of the challenges he was set, he would find himself on the road to success. But if his tutors broke his spirit and he failed, they'd consider the clan well rid of him. More was always asked of those with more to offer.

Seba had no time to comfort or reassure his struggling assistant. The job of quartermaster was more demanding than he had imagined and his first few years were a hectic period of adjustment. There were so many details he had to stay on top of, from cultivating luminous lichen in tunnels where the glowing moss had died out, to maintaining the stocks of live animals, to ensuring coffins were kept clean for visitors, to dealing with the eerie Guardians of the Blood.

When Larten was injured and unable to train, he sometimes assisted Seba. It was while helping his master that he came to learn about the Guardians. He had always assumed that the blood in Vampire Mountain was shipped in and stored in vats, but now he found that most of it came from a tribe of humans living in the bowels of the mountain.

The Guardians were pale, strange creatures. In exchange for their blood, they took care of certain burial details when a vampire died, extracting each corpse's inner organs and brains, draining its body dry. Many vampires chose to be sent down a mountain stream when they died. If their corpses weren't fully cleaned out in advance, animals would feast on their poisonous organs and go insane.

Larten didn't like the Guardians – they had an aloof air and seldom answered if spoken to – but he wanted to learn as much as he could about the clan and its workings, so he studied them as dispassionately as possible.

Memorising facts about the clan was also part of his training. Vampires were expected to familiarise themselves with their history, learn the names of their past leaders, be able to recite the many legends of their gods. Most vampires were illiterate. Books were for humans, not children of the night. Their history was recorded in tales and legends, passed on by word of mouth, and all had to help sustain it. If a disease or war ever wiped out the majority of the clan, the few who were left could at least keep their origins, achievements and myths alive.

Larten learnt much about his race. Those were the nights he looked forward to most, when he and the other trainees sat around and listened to their elders wax lyrical about the past or chant ancient songs. He had a keen memory and was able to recount most of what he heard. Wester was even smarter and stored away details which Larten couldn't retain, but his friend had always been mentally sharper, so Larten didn't mind lagging behind in that department.

Wester was most interested in stories about the vampaneze. Many Generals would have happily made no mention of the breakaway group, but the war that had erupted subsequently was a crucial part of their heritage, so they reluctantly discussed the reasons behind the split and what the other night creatures had been doing since then.

Wester wanted to find out everything he could

about the vampaneze and he never seemed satisfied with what the Generals told him. He began sidetracking vampires in the Halls and tunnels, asking questions and learning more about their foes. He fell in with a group of vampaneze haters. Each of them thought that the purple-skinned traitors should be hunted to extinction. They respected the rule of the Princes — that went without question — but schemed on the sly, keeping abreast of vampaneze movements and activities, in case their leaders ever decided to sanction another war.

Wester tried to involve Larten with his new network of friends. He invited Larten to meetings and urged him to listen to their tales of vampaneze atrocities. Because Larten thought of Wester as a brother, he met with the disgruntled vampires and listened quietly as they spun wild stories of vampaneze drinking the blood of babies and targeting royals and politicians in human society. According to the rumours, they were establishing contacts around the globe, gathering an army of humans to support them in a strike on Vampire Mountain.

"They'll kill us all if we don't hit them first!" was the common rallying cry.

Larten dismissed the speculation and urged Wester to do the same. "They are mad, the lot of them," he argued. Then, before Wester could refute that, he said, "No, not all. Some speak truly, those who simply report on what the vampaneze do and where they travel. But these tales of armies and master plans…" He snorted. "The vampaneze have nothing but scorn for humans. They see mankind as cattle to drain and discard. One of the reasons they broke away from us was because of our leniency. They mock us for not killing when we feed. To suggest that they are working in league with humans is a lie and one that can easily be exposed. Question the *conspirators*. Vampaneze always tell the truth. Ask them if they plot against us. They will answer honestly — and answer nay."

"Don't tell me you believe that old tale," Wester sneered. "Of course they lie. They just want us to think that they don't."

Larten realised he and Wester would never see eye to eye on this matter. To avoid arguments – and maybe a fight, since Wester felt that strongly about it – he stopped mingling with the dissidents. Whenever Wester invited him to a meeting, Larten made an excuse not to go. Wester soon acknowledged his friend's wishes and cut Larten out of that part of his life. He cut out his master too, knowing in his heart that although Seba disliked those who had split from the clan, he would never urge war against them. The old vampire might welcome a war if it came to pass, but he wouldn't try to provoke one or approve of those who did.

Seba would have been worried if he'd seen the vampires Wester was involved with. Maybe he would have urged his hot-headed ward to stay out of such complex, dangerous affairs. But the quartermaster was still adjusting to his new position and had little time to focus on his assistants. He kept up with reports of their development, but other than that he trusted them to the guiding hands of their tutors. By the time Seba settled into his job and was able to pay closer attention to his charges, Wester had learnt not to discuss his feelings except with those who felt the same way he did.

Larten could have told Seba what was happening, but he didn't think it was important. Wester and his allies respected the rule of the Princes, there was no doubt about that, so he saw no real threat in their angry mutterings. As long as the vampire leaders maintained the truce, dissenters like Wester could do nothing to cause trouble. They were bound by their sense of duty, the way every vampire was. At worst they could march off to perish in the wilderness, as Perta Vin-Grahl and his supporters once had.

But Larten was sure it wouldn't come to that. They

were just letting off steam, all talk and bluster. Nothing would come of their scaremongering. They'd need the backing of a Prince to move forward with their plans of war, but what vampire of high standing would ever support a crazy, bloodthirsty cause like theirs?

CHAPTER THIRTEEN

Larten's mood had darkened steadily. He was growing more disillusioned with every passing night and had come to hate his training, Vampire Mountain, the hierarchy of Generals and Princes. It all seemed pointless. What could they achieve, cut off from the world, never interfering in the ways of humans, settling for the shadows instead of controlling the night?

He had been looking forward to Council – he'd spent long hours practising one-armed combat in the months leading up to it, anticipating his rematch with the broken-nosed General – but even that proved disappointing. He enjoyed the fighting and games, but every vampire seemed full of disquieting tales. Mankind was making massive industrial advances. Cities were growing at a dizzying rate. Men were dominating the planet more than ever before. Vampires were having to withdraw deep into the wilds to roam freely.

There was an air of crisis about that Council. Two

new Princes had been elected, but the clan felt as if they were at a crossroads and didn't know which way to turn. There was no sense of direction from their leaders — the Princes were divided on the issue of how to respond to the changing world. Seba had seen indecision like this before, so he took little notice of the alarm, confident that time would iron out the creases, that vampires would adapt as they always had. But to Larten it seemed like the clan was unravelling, that he was wasting his time training to be a member of an outdated order.

While Larten flailed, Wester had found a new calling and was fully focused on it. After a long talk with Seba, he had realised the life of a General wasn't for him. What he relished was life in Vampire Mountain. Abandoning his training, he instead started studying to become a guard. While they weren't as highly respected as Generals – no guard had ever become a Prince – it was an important position and Larten was happy for his friend. He suspected Wester would make a fine guard and might one night replace Seba as quartermaster. He was pleased that Wester had chosen a suitable path and was forging ahead.

But it also made him more unsure of his own route. He couldn't say with all honesty that he still wanted to be a General. He'd had doubts before Council and they increased afterwards. Was he pursuing this course simply because it would make Seba happy? He had no idea what he would do if he quit — was uncertainty about his future the only reason he continued to study?

In the months and years after Council his unhappiness festered. Joy seeped from his life and he went about his training half-heartedly, taking no joy from his successes, learning nothing from his failures. Seba saw the gloom that the young vampire had succumbed to. He had more time for his assistants now, but Larten was distant around his master. Seba tried getting him to talk about his depression, but Larten rebuffed all advances.

Seba desperately wanted to help his troubled charge. He would have done anything to bring a smile to Larten's face. But he was helpless. Larten had to make the first move. Change was essential, but only the trainee General had the power to take his life by the scruff of the neck and shake it up.

Then, one night, thanks to a cluster of dead vampires, he did.

The Guardians of the Blood informed Seba of the problem, sending one of their pale members to track him down. Seba had been aware of the stench – most of the vampires in the mountain had caught a whiff of it – but there had been similar cases in the past and each time the issue had resolved itself. But the Guardian said that this was different. They needed to sort it out.

Seba summoned a team and had them meet him in the Hall of Final Voyage, a small cave with a stream flowing through it. This was where many vampires over the centuries had chosen to be cast off when they died. The stream would carry their bodies down through the hidden tunnels of the mountain, then wash them out into the world and far away. The custom was dying out – cremation was the current popular trend – but some of the elder vampires still preferred the more traditional method.

"I trust you can all smell that," Seba said cheerfully once his crew was in place. He took a deep breath of the putrid air and smiled as if sniffing perfume.

"I thought it was Goulder," someone laughed.

"Shut your mouth or I'll shut it for you," a vampire named Patrick Goulder snapped. Larten and the others covered their smiles. Patrick did have a problem with his odour, but it was nowhere near as bad as this.

"Bodies are stuck in the tunnel," Seba said. "This is not the first time it has happened. Usually, when the water rises in winter, it washes them away. But the Guardians have told me that will not happen on this occasion. We have to go down there and free them."

The vampires frowned, then a few looked to Larten with their eyebrows raised. Since he was Seba's assistant, it was his place to ask the question going through all of their minds.

"Surely this is a job for the Guardians," Larten muttered. "They are in charge of burials."

"No," Seba said. "*We* are in charge. We let them take control of certain details because it suits our needs. But this is our problem, not theirs.

"Come now," he chortled, trying to raise their spirits. "It is not that bad. I have brought pegs for your noses and you will be tied to one another with ropes to ensure that none of you gets washed away. The water is no colder than in the Hall of Perta Vin-Grahl. Our chefs have prepared a fine broth for when you return. It will be an adventure!"

"Are you going down the tunnel, Seba?" one of the team asked.

"I would love to," Seba sighed. "But my back…" He winced and held his sides like an old woman.

The vampires laughed and started roping themselves together. Some would stay with Seba, to hold the ropes and pull back the others if the current proved too strong. But Larten was one of those charged with wading down the tunnel.

Larten shivered as he lowered himself into the fast-flowing water. Partly it was the chill, but mostly it was the eerie feeling of staring directly into the mouth of the funereal tunnel. Larten had never expected to pass through this opening alive. It was a journey only the dead were meant to take. It felt wrong, as if he and the others were trespassing, going where the living weren't welcome.

"I know this is difficult," Seba said seriously, "but you have nothing to fear. There are no ghosts. All of the vampires who passed through here were of good standing. Their souls flew directly to Paradise when they died."

The team in the water hesitated despite Seba's reassurances, staring down that awful hole at the blackness. Then Larten, since he knew that Seba would expect it of him, clapped loudly. "Move on there!" he shouted at the vampires ahead of him. "The sooner we finish this, the sooner we can be back in the Hall of Khledon Lurt, warming up with a bowl of broth and a mug of ale."

Cheers greeted that and the vampires in the lead — there were two teams, set side by side — released their grip on the bank and let the current carry them out of the cave and into darkness.

Each team had a torch-carrier, but they came at the rear. So, when Larten entered the tunnel, he had to endure a minute of near-total gloom. He imagined lonely spirits drifting around him and was almost afraid of what the light of the torches would reveal. But, as Seba had said, there were no ghosts here. When the torch-bearers finally lit up the area, Larten saw nothing except rock and water. Offering up a quick prayer to the gods, he moved on in search of the blockage.

The stench worsened as they advanced and the pegs on their noses didn't help much. It seemed to thicken in the air around them and soak into their pores. A couple of the vampires choked and were sick. The teams paused to let the vomit float ahead of them. Larten could feel his own insides rumbling, but he managed to keep his food down.

They inched their way along the tunnel, the team in the cave keeping a tight rein on them. Nobody knew what lay ahead. If the floor suddenly dropped into an underground waterfall, those on the ropes didn't want the others being swept away. As impatient as the vampires in the tunnel were, Seba made sure that the team in the cave kept a firm grip on the rope and fed it out at a slow, steady rate. Larten had no idea if he'd been in the water ten minutes or an hour. All he knew was that it seemed like an age.

Eventually they came to where the bodies had stacked up and it was far worse than anyone had imagined. Larten tried to count the corpses, but it was impossible. They were rammed tight, a wall of bones and rotting flesh. Some were skeletons – this had been building for a number of years – but most were dotted with scraps of skin and hair. Larten could probably have recognised some of the dead if he'd looked closely.

He didn't.

Gagging and pale-faced, they closed in on the wall of the dead. One of the vampires near the front screamed and had to be released. Clinging to the rope, he scuttled back to the safety of the cave. Larten should have felt contempt, but all he could muster was envy. He wanted to follow the coward and it took all of his willpower not to.

Larten watched sickly as the two vampires at the head of the team reached out and tugged at the obstruction. If luck was with the group, the pair at the front would shake the corpses free and the rest of them need never touch the remains of the dead.

But the luck of the vampires was in scarce supply that night. The wall of bones rattled but didn't give. Sighing, Larten and the others edged forward until all were within touching distance of the stinking corpses.

Patrick Goulder raised a fist and threw a punch at the bones nearest him, trying to smash a way through.

"Stop!" Larten roared. When Patrick looked at him, Larten growled, "They might be dead, but they are still children of the clan, Generals who fought bravely and deserve our respect. We will not shatter their bones unless all else fails. We will try to pry them apart gently, to keep each corpse intact."

Patrick snorted. "Do you think it makes a difference? They'll be torn to pieces by animals on the outside anyway."

"What happens outside is not our business," Larten said. "What happens within this mountain *is*."

Patrick rolled his eyes but didn't argue. Since Larten had spoken up and taken charge, it fell on him to make the first stab at the mound of bodies. Gulping, he reached up, ran his fingers over a few of the skeletons, located the shoulders of one and pulled softly. When nothing happened, he tugged harder. Finally the upper half came free, but so did a mess of rotting bat corpses that had lodged in the network of bones. They shot out of a hole that Larten hadn't seen, propelled by a snapping bone, and splattered his face.

Larten shrieked, fell backwards and went under, pulling the skeleton with him. For a moment of pure panic he thrashed beneath the water, the bones of the dead pushing him down. He thought the vampire had come back to life and was trying to kill him. He lashed out at the bones, tasting the foulness of the dead bats. He tried to spit them out, but water drove disgusting bits of organs back into his throat. As Larten retched, hands gripped his arms and pulled him up.

He cried out as he broke the surface, eyes wild. The peg had been knocked from his nose and the stench hit him harder than ever. He retched again, vomiting up the contents of his stomach.

"Do you want to go back?" Patrick Goulder asked.

Larten wanted to retreat more than anything. But it would have been a sign of weakness and he didn't want to lose face in front of the others.

"Just give me a minute," he gasped, wiping his lips clean and letting his heart settle. When the tremble in his hands subsided slightly, he joined the rest of the team and went to work on the bodies again.

They spent most of the next hour in the cold, wet confines of the tunnel, freeing bones and limbs, picking intertwined skeletons apart, carefully loosening the knot of bodies. It was hard, horrible work, and they did it in silence. Each of them knew that they would never discuss this afterwards. This wasn't a dirty job which they'd make light of later. It was an awful task and it would haunt them for many weeks and months to come. No amount of ale would erode this unpleasant memory. Larten had a nasty suspicion that he might even take it with him to the grave.

CHAPTER FOURTEEN

When the crew in the tunnel returned solemn and grim, nobody tried to lighten the atmosphere. Seba and the vampires on the ropes could see the horror in the eyes of those they dragged back. Without saying anything they covered the sodden team in blankets and led them to where broth, bread and ale were waiting in abundance.

Larten ate mechanically, filling the emptiness of his stomach, eyes unfocused. He was thinking about the corpses, imagining himself as one of them. Vampires could live for hundreds of years. Most rarely thought about time the way humans did, since they had so much of it to play with. Death was a far-off, distant thing for the average child of the night.

But the bodies in the tunnel had reminded Larten of his mortality. There was no guarantee that he would live to be as old as Seba. Maybe destiny would strike him down young. If it did, he wanted to be able to say that he had truly lived, that he had experienced all of the pleasures of the world, that he hadn't just trudged along miserably like a turtle in the shell of Vampire Mountain.

Larten didn't even touch his mug of ale. In a corner of his mind he had already made his decision, and although he hadn't consciously realised that yet, part of him made sure that he kept a clear head. When he acted, that part wanted him to be sober, so there could be no doubt that he meant it.

He was halfway through a second bowl of broth when he stopped, pushed it aside and stood. The others glanced at him but said nothing. He wasn't the first to depart the table abruptly. They assumed he was leaving to be sick. But they were wrong.

Larten made a beeline for Seba's cave. The quartermaster had his own room in the mountain. He'd offered to share it with his assistants, but they had declined — Seba was now a vampire of great importance and he was entitled to his privacy.

Wester was with their master, discussing some matter to do with his training. Larten was relieved — it meant he'd just have to go through this once. It was only years later that he wondered if Seba had read the intention in his eyes when he was pulled out of the tunnel, even before he knew of it himself, and summoned Wester on a pretext to make things easier for Larten.

If Seba *did* know what Larten was going to say, he hid the knowledge well. There was nothing in his expression but mild curiosity when Larten entered. "Can I help you?" he asked politely.

"I am leaving," Larten said.

Wester stared at him oddly. He knew nothing of the pile-up in the tunnel or what Larten had been through. But Seba knew what his assistant meant and he nodded softly. "Very well."

Larten frowned. "You do not understand. I am quitting my studies. I do not want to be a General. I am sick of this place. I am *leaving*."

"No!" Wester gasped. "You can't mean it. What's happened? Why are you—"

"I understand perfectly," Seba interrupted. "I never asked you to stay and I do not hold you against your will. You are no longer a Cub. You are a man of wisdom and experience. I am honoured that you and Wester still call me master, but in truth no one is your master now or ever will be again. If you wish to go, you can go with my blessings."

Larten hadn't expected this. In a strange way he felt cheated. He wanted Seba to be hurt, to try and convince him to stay. It was childish – *human* – but in his heart he craved attention. This was a momentous decision and he needed an argument to mark it.

Wester unwittingly gave Larten what he required.

"You can't leave," he huffed. "This is madness. Seba told me you've nearly completed your training."

"I also asked you to keep that information to yourself," Seba snapped, eyes flashing with a rare spike of anger.

"Is that true?" Larten asked, momentarily flustered. He had thought he was five or ten years away from becoming a General, assuming he passed his tests at all.

"You have impressed some of your peers," Seba sniffed, still glaring at Wester. "There was talk of passing you in the near future. But after this display, I doubt it. A General must know his mind completely. On this evidence, you do not."

"I damn well do," Larten growled, finding his fury again. "I want out. I do not want to be a General. You are all old-fashioned and backwards."

"Larten!" Wester cried, alarmed by this vicious, uncharacteristic attack.

Larten laughed bitterly. "Every vampire should pursue his dreams, live life to its maximum, chase a glorious, savage death. We should not be imprisoned here, *training*. Are we students or men? Humans or vampires?"

Before Wester could answer, Larten pressed on. "I say to hell with Generals, Princes and the rest. Life is too short. I want to live, fight, love, die. Not waste my time studying."

"Who is stopping you?" Seba thundered. He had been sitting, but now he rose and faced Larten on his feet. His cheeks were flushed. "If we disgust you, leave immediately. Do not even pause to pack your belongings — you can do without them. I never intended to come between you and your *dreams*." He invested the word with as much sarcasm as he could.

"Very well," Larten snarled. "I will."

And with that he stormed out of the room. Wester gave a cry and darted after Larten, but Seba grabbed him as he tried to pass.

"No," Seba said quietly. "Leave him be."

"But we can't let him run off like that!" Wester exclaimed. "He wasn't thinking clearly. He'll be sorry when he calms down. He'll want to apologise. We have to let him know—"

"He was more himself in that outburst than he has been for many years," Seba said, then chuckled. Wester was astonished to see his master smiling.

"Larten needs to go," Seba said, sitting again and narrowing his eyes. He was imagining the path the young vampire would take, the tunnels he'd hurry through, the thoughts that might be crashing around inside his head. He hoped Larten would stay true to his convictions — it would be disastrous if he turned back now.

"Master... I don't understand... don't you like Larten any more?"

"Like him?" Seba's features softened. "I love him, you idiot, as I love you. You are sons to me, as I have told you before. But every son must put considerations of his father aside eventually. You did that when you chose to train to be a guard — you made a choice and became your own man. Larten is doing the same."

"But he left in such a foul temper. Perhaps I should call him back and—"

"By the gods, no!" Seba shouted. "You are wiser than that, Wester Flack, so do not act like a fool. I know you will miss Larten – I will too – but it is time for him to seek his own way. If you interfere now, you might destroy him. This has been a difficult decision for him to make. If he relented, returned and had to make the choice again later, I do not think that he could."

"But..." Wester stared at his master. "What if I went with him?"

"You have the same right to leave as he has," Seba said stiffly. Then he smiled. "But you will not. Your place is here and you know it. We must let him go. If the luck of the vampires is with him, he will return when he is ready. But for now he must walk his own path, or at least try to find it."

Wester nodded slowly, then looked at the gaping space of the doorway. "I fear for him. He doesn't know what he wants. He'll run into trouble."

"Probably," Seba said glumly. "But he is strong and I believe that he will find his way in the end. If I am wrong…" Seba sighed and pressed the middle finger of his left hand to his forehead. Keeping his eyes open, he covered them with his second and fourth fingers, spreading his thumb and smallest finger wide. "Even in death may he be triumphant."

Then Seba put all thoughts of his departing assistant from his mind and focused on his duties, leaving Larten Crepsley to the unknowable workings of whatever destiny held in store for him.

PART FOUR

"I can stitch you up if you wish."

CHAPTER FIFTEEN

The next few years of Larten Crepsley's life were his wildest and most carefree. Larten flitted to get away swiftly from all that he had come to loathe, even though vampires were not supposed to flit on the path to or from the mountain. The rebellious act was his way of showing how little he cared for the rules of the clan. He knew it was a petty gesture, but that didn't stop him.

He cut through the world at a frenetic pace, travelling freely, spending much of his time on boats, carriages, even trains. It was his first time trying one of the iron horses. The rocking motion made him feel sick to begin with, but he adjusted to it after a while, even though he never wavered from his opinion that it went far faster than any land vehicle had a need to.

For years he avoided contact with other vampires, moving from one town and city to another, mixing mostly with men of lax principles and ladies of easy virtue, since they were the ones who came out at night. He stole vast amounts of money and spent it lavishly. He gambled heavily, backed many foolish, high-risk ventures for sport, and at one stage ran his own stable of boxers and fighting cockerels.

Larten tried things he'd avoided even as a Cub, things no sane person should try. He treated his body with disrespect, interested only in how far he could push it. There were many nights when he couldn't rise, only lie in a dark room, shaking like a rabid rat, waiting for death to put him out of his misery.

If he had been a lesser vampire, he would have surely died. But his years of harsh lessons had toughened him. He could take more punishment than most, go further, last longer. No matter how many mad nights he subjected himself to, he always struggled back.

In time he calmed down and put the worst of the craziness behind him. He had tasted almost all the dark pleasures of the human world and was bored of them. He made no friends in those seedy years, but many cronies flocked to his side, men and women all too eager to spend the money he never seemed to run out of, to go on wild sprees with him and try to match his wild appetites. They praised Larten and spoke of their love and respect for him, but he knew they were lost, base creatures, wringing what profit they could from one in an even worse state than themselves.

One night he simply walked out on the hangers-on, the same way he had walked out on the clan. They were much easier to leave behind than Seba or Wester. These people didn't truly care for him, only for the wicked pleasures he brought into their lives. They were vermin and vultures. He didn't think he was any better than them, but he hoped that he could be. Out of pity, he threw what cash he had at them and left while they squabbled over it.

He tried running with the Cubs again. There was a gaping hole in his life that needed to be filled. He craved company and excitement. He didn't want to wake every evening by himself, bored, lonely, desperate to kill time. He yearned to find a purpose and he thought the Cubs might give him that, at least for a time.

But going back to the war packs was a mistake. All of the vampires he'd known had moved on or died. Their replacements welcomed Larten into the fold, but he felt awkward around them. He couldn't work up the same enthusiasm for drink, war, women and gambling. He found the young Cubs loud, ignorant and dull. He didn't like to believe he'd ever been so shallow, but was sure he must have been.

He fed with war packs a couple of times, then no more. Bidding the Cubs a not-so-fond farewell, he wandered again, keeping to himself, avoiding the larger towns and crowds. He spent many lonely nights in graveyards or caves, brooding, feeling as if he would never find his place in the world.

Returning to the Cirque Du Freak, he asked Mr Tall if he could help out as he had before. Hibernius Tall wasn't one to turn away an old friend, but Larten soon realised this wasn't the life for him, certainly not in his current state. He loved the circus and would have been happy at another time to settle down there. But he was restless, so he moved on with no more idea of what he wanted than he had when he left Vampire Mountain.

A few years after that, Larten was hunting deer. He had been tracking a herd for hours. He could have moved in for the kill sooner, but he was in no rush. His clothes were filthy rags. He'd grown a beard – a light brown colour, which must have been the original shade of his hair – and his nails were long and ragged. There were blood stains around his mouth from previous feasts and dried-in smears across his cheeks.

"Charna's guts! You look even rougher than me," someone laughed behind him, startling the vampire. He twirled so fast that he lost his balance and fell. As he landed on his backside, his gaze settled on a grinning Vancha March.

"What are you doing here?" Larten barked.

"Just happened to be passing," Vancha sniffed. "I caught your smell — couldn't really miss it — and thought I'd come see what you were up to."

Vancha spent the next couple of nights roaming with Larten, letting him tell his sorry story. The General made no comment, just listened quietly. When Larten finally ran out of words to express his miserable state, Vancha said that the younger vampire could travel with him if he wished.

"I'm going through a bit of an aimless period myself," he said. "I went on a quest to find the palace of Perta Vin-Grahl a few years ago." Vin-Grahl had led a group of vampires off into a frozen wilderness to die not long after the war with the vampaneze. According to legends, they'd built a castle of ice and turned it into a mass burial tomb. Many vampires had searched for the last resting place of the doomed group over the centuries.

"Any luck?" Larten asked.

"No," Vancha sighed. "I really thought I'd find it, but all I got in the end was frostbite. Almost lost a few toes. I've been too ashamed to report back to the clan. I can't avoid them indefinitely, but I'd like to wait a bit longer before subjecting myself to their laughter. Paris will be especially tickled — he bet me my favourite shuriken that I wouldn't find the palace."

The pair wandered purposelessly but pleasantly for the next year. They hunted and told each other stories. They regularly sparred to pass the time and Larten unwittingly found himself completing many of the tasks he would have had to pass to become a General. Vancha would always swear blind over the decades to come that he hadn't meant to play the part of a mentor, but Larten had his doubts. Like Seba, Vancha could be a sly operator when slyness was called for.

Most nights they slept beneath a tree or bush. Vancha didn't believe in creature comforts like coffins. He was never happier than when sleeping on a cold, rocky floor, covered in nothing more than his purple animal hides. Larten didn't enjoy such lean living, but he got used to it. In any case, it was better to sleep rough with a friend than in the lap of luxury by himself.

One night, while resting, Vancha decided to show off his spitting prowess. He spat high into the air, kept his mouth open and caught the spit as it dropped back down. Gulping, he chortled and said, "I bet you can't do that."

"Why in the name of all the gods would I want to?" Larten muttered.

"It's a talent," Vancha said.

"So is picking your nose with your tongue."

"Can you?" Vancha asked eagerly.

"I have never tried and I do not intend to," Larten said.

Vancha stuck out his tongue and explored, but although he could touch the tip of his nose if he pushed it down with a finger, his tongue wouldn't reach as far as his nostril of its own accord. In the end he grunted and settled for spitting high and catching it again.

"Come on," he urged Larten. "Try it. It's fun."

"I have no intention of spitting on myself," Larten said stiffly, smothering a smile. "Now leave me alone or you will be swallowing one of your shurikens instead of a gobful of spit."

"Leave my shurikens alone," Vancha growled, caressing the throwing stars that were attached to belts looped around his body. Vancha preferred to fight with his hands – he believed weapons were a sign of weakness – but the shurikens were an exception. "Some of these are hundreds of years old. They're historical."

Larten frowned. "I thought you made them yourself."

"Most of them, aye. But I've got several from the early decades of the Edo Period, and even one that I think goes back to the Kamakuras."

"What are you talking about?" Larten asked.

"The great Japanese dynasties. Don't you know anything of history?"

"Not a lot," Larten said. "I spent the last thirty or so years trying to memorise all of the vampire milestones. I had no time to research human history too."

"You should have made time," Vancha tutted. "Only a fool forgets where he comes from. I don't have much to do with the human world, but we all started off there and we can learn much about ourselves by studying the highs and lows of mankind over the centuries."

"Then tell me, good master," Larten simpered. Although he was being sarcastic, Vancha took the request seriously. For the next few nights Larten was treated to a full rundown of the Japanese dynasties from the Asuka up to the Edo, with special emphasis on the weapons each favoured, particularly those of the small, pointed, throwing kind. By the end of his lessons, he almost wished he *had* followed through on his threat and rammed a shuriken down Vancha's throat. The shabby, smelly General was a fine friend, but a truly boring historian!

CHAPTER SIXTEEN

Eventually Vancha had to resume his duties. As a General he had to sit in on various meetings, keep an eye on the Cubs, monitor the movements of the vampaneze, investigate rogue vampires. He invited Larten to join him on a few assignments. Since he had nothing better to do, Larten accepted.

Having checked on a few of the rowdier Cubs and admonished them – even the tearaway youngsters were expected to obey certain rules – Vancha and Larten set off in pursuit of a vampire called Arrow who had severed contact with the clan. The Princes wanted to know why he had cut himself off.

Vancha found their target by a process known as triangulation. Like almost every vampire, Arrow had placed his hands on the Stone of Blood in Vampire Mountain when he'd pledged himself to the clan, allowing it to draw blood from him. One of the Princes in the mountain checked with the magical

Stone and located Arrow's position. The Prince then communicated telepathically with Vancha and directed him.

Vancha followed his directions until they came to a house in a forest. They arrived late at night and made camp without approaching the house. After a short sleep, they lurked behind a couple of trees and kept watch throughout the day. They saw a red-haired woman at work within and around the house over the course of the day, but there was no sign of Arrow.

He appeared as the sun was setting. He came out, squinted at the sky, kissed the woman then went to get water as she slipped inside the house. Arrow was a large, bald, thickly built man. There were tattoos of arrows on both sides of his head and down his forearms. He didn't look like someone who would walk away the worse for wear from most fights. His scowl as he drew a bucket of water from a well to the side of the house did nothing to soften his tough impression.

Arrow set the full bucket on the ground beside the well then growled without looking up. "Come forward if you're coming. I don't like peeping Thomases."

"Apologies," Vancha said airily, stepping out into sight. "I wasn't sure what the state of play was. Didn't want to barge in and create any difficulties."

Arrow nodded gruffly at Vancha, ran a cold eye over Larten, then sniffed. "Sarah will have dinner ready soon. You're welcome to share it with us."

Larten and Vancha exchanged a glance, then moved forward. Vancha looked relaxed, but Larten noted the way his fingers stayed by his shurikens. He made sure his knives were within easy reach and kept close to Vancha, ready to back him up if they were attacked.

The woman inside the house – Sarah – looked up with surprise when Arrow stomped in and said, "We have visitors." She started to smile curiously when the odd pair entered. Then Arrow said, "They're vampires." Her smile vanished in an instant and she set the table in silence.

Arrow laid the bucket close to the fire, kissed Sarah again, then sat and nodded for Vancha and Larten to join him. "Sarah's my wife," he said quietly, his hands clenched into fists. "Where does the clan stand on such issues these nights?"

"You married a human?" Vancha frowned.

"I married a beautiful, loving woman," Arrow corrected him. Larten saw a smile dart across Sarah's lips as she half turned to look at her husband. "Now answer my question."

Vancha scratched an armpit. "You weren't this grumpy before. The soft life doesn't agree with you."

"It agreed with me nicely until you and your assistant turned up," Arrow said.

"Larten's not my assistant, just a friend."

"No matter. I've asked twice already, Vancha. Don't make me–"

"The Generals aren't interested," Vancha said. "We don't approve of vampires mating with humans, but it's been a long time since we banned such unions, so why are you worried?"

"Times change," Arrow noted. "I wasn't sure what the current mood was. When you turned up, after I'd asked to be left alone, I thought–"

"Slow down," Vancha interrupted. "Who did you *ask?* You dropped out of sight without a word to anyone. That's why I came."

Arrow frowned. "I told Azis Bendetta of my decision when I chose to abandon my studies and not become a General."

Vancha sighed. "Azis is dead."

"When?"

"Four years or more."

"Even in death may he be triumphant," Arrow muttered, making the death's touch sign. He looked sad as he lowered his hand, but relieved too. "He must have died before he delivered my message."

"Aye." Vancha was smiling now.

"So I'm not in any trouble?"

"No."

Arrow shook his head and chuckled, then boomed, "Sarah! Ale and warm milk for our guests."

"I'll take mine cold, thanks," Vancha laughed, then leant forward and clapped Arrow's shoulder. When Larten saw that, he relaxed and smiled at Sarah as she passed him a mug of ale. When no one was looking, he shifted his knives around to the side. This wasn't to be a night for fighting after all.

Arrow's story was short and simple. He had met Sarah and fallen in love. He'd told her the truth about himself early in their relationship, that he was a barren, bloodsucking night creature who would live for hundreds of years.

"His sterility was the hardest thing to accept," Sarah said. She had a soft voice and a shy smile. "I wasn't worried about the vampire part – I could tell he wasn't evil – and I'm glad he'll live so long. But not being able to have children…"

"We'll probably take in some orphans one day," Arrow said, rubbing a finger down Sarah's arm. "But at the moment we're still enjoying being a couple. The novelty hasn't worn off yet. We'll start a family in a few years, aye?"

"Aye," Sarah giggled.

It wasn't unheard of for a vampire to take a human mate, but usually only Cubs crossed that divide.

"Five years ago I'd have said you were crazy if you'd told me this would happen," Arrow insisted. "I didn't approve of those who mated outside the—"

"Arrow..." Sarah said warningly.

"Sorry. Those who *married* outside the clan."

"What's wrong with mating?" Vancha asked.

"Animals mate," Sarah said frostily. "Humans marry."

"But we're neither," Vancha noted.

"You're more human than animal," Sarah said. "At least Arrow and Larten are." She cocked an eyebrow at the odd-looking, green-haired vampire and he hooted with delight. To Vancha, an insult from a beautiful woman counted as a twisted compliment.

"Anyway," Arrow went on, "I was content as a General. I never meant to look for a human mate — wife," he corrected himself quickly as Sarah narrowed her eyes. "But we met while I was recovering from a wound and..." He shrugged.

"...you lived happily ever after," Vancha finished with a smile. Then his smile faded. "Except you won't, will you? Forgive me for speaking bluntly, Sarah, but human lives are short compared to ours. Do you plan to let Arrow blood you?"

"No," Sarah said with conviction. "I love the sun too much to hide from it. I'd rather a short life of days than centuries of nights."

"So what happens when your heart gives out and Arrow has to stick you in a hole to rot?" Vancha asked.

"As diplomatic as ever," Arrow said drily, sharing a sad look with his wife.

"That worries me," Sarah whispered, grasping Arrow's hand. "I almost didn't marry him because I don't want to leave him like that, but…"

"The future will bring what it brings," Arrow grunted. "There are no guarantees in life. I might die before her, of disease or an accident. If I don't, I will grieve as any husband grieves when his wife dies. Then… I'm not sure. If we have children, I'll finish rearing them. If we have grandchildren, I might stay and watch them grow. If not, or after that… who knows?"

"The clan will welcome you back if you choose to return," Vancha said. "We won't cut you off just because you fell in love. You can finish your training – you were only months away from your final test, and you know we all thought highly of you."

"That's kind of you, but I can't see myself ever being a General now. Maybe that will change, but I doubt it. Perhaps, if I outlive her, I'll just sit by Sarah's grave, drink no blood and wait to join her."

"You'll do no such thing!" Sarah barked. "If you do, and there's a Paradise, I'll make your life a misery for the rest of eternity."

Arrow leant forward and kissed her flushed forehead. "Whatever you say, my dear," he murmured.

They stayed up late, eating, drinking, chatting. Sarah went to bed a few hours before sunrise and then it was just the vampires. When they were alone, they spoke of the clan. Vancha told Arrow about Azis Bendetta's death and brought him up to date with all the latest intrigues and happenings.

"The anti-vampaneze brigade is going strong," he said at one point. "The fools are spoiling for a war. As if one wasn't enough."

"Do you really think it might come to that?" Arrow asked, alarmed.

"No," Vancha said. "The Princes know that war would be catastrophic. One or two might be swayed if the situation was different, but as long as there are the likes of Paris and Chok Yamada to talk sense to them, the truce will hold."

They slept in Arrow's house that day – Vancha reluctantly made his bed on the soft (by his standards) wooden floor, not wanting to offend his host by sleeping outside – and ate with him and Sarah the following night. After their meal, Vancha wished the

pair the luck of the vampires, then he and Larten took
their leave.

Larten was thoughtful as they slipped through the
forest. He'd never considered returning to the human
fold as Arrow had. Part of him liked the idea of finding
a mate, marrying, adopting children. He'd thought
that he had left that world behind forever, but now he
saw that it could be his again if he truly wanted it.

"That's a waste of a good vampire," Vancha sighed,
disturbing Larten's train of thought. "Arrow was a
great fighter. He could have gone far."

"But he is happy where he is," Larten noted.

Vancha shrugged. "Since when did vampires care
about happiness? A creature of the night feels satisfied
when all is well with his world. That's nature's way.
Happiness is a human folly. Vampires who seek it
usually come to no good."

"That is a cynical way of looking at life," Larten
said.

"I call it like I see it," Vancha huffed. "If Arrow had
taken a vampiress for a mate, that would be different.
But marrying a human..." He shook his head then
chuckled. "Mind you, having cast my eye over the
vampiresses at the last Council, I can't blame him.
They're a grim lot, aren't they? Fine fighters, but you
wouldn't want to kiss any of them!"

"I do not think that someone in your position can be too particular," Larten said.

"What are you talking about?" Vancha frowned. "I'd be a first-rate catch. No woman could go wrong with a specimen like me." To prove his point, he spat into his palm and wiped phlegm into his scalp. "I mean, seriously, what lady of taste could resist a shiny, green head of hair like mine?"

CHAPTER SEVENTEEN

Soon after their meeting with Arrow, Vancha was summoned to Vampire Mountain on business. Larten chose not to travel with him. They made vague plans to meet up again, but their paths took them elsewhere and several years passed without any contact.

Larten spent those years falling back into the dark pit from which Vancha had briefly rescued him. His time with the General had refired his love for the clan, reminding him why he'd agreed to become Seba's assistant in the first place. But he still didn't want to return to Vampire Mountain and complete his training. Not yet. He had a sense that he wasn't finished with the human world, that until he worked whatever was troubling him out of his system, he would never know peace.

One night as he glumly considered his options – trying to pick a country or city he hadn't visited before – he found himself thinking about Lady Evanna.

He hadn't thought of the witch in a long time. He'd meant to take advantage of her offer to visit her at home, but it had slipped his mind.

He knew instantly that this was what he craved. Something different, a place neither part of the human nor vampire world. He had no idea where Evanna lived, but he was sure he could find her. She'd given him that ability. All he had to do was set off and his feet would lead him.

It was a long trek. He had meant to use trains and carriages, but whenever he got on one he lost track of where he was going. Flitting disoriented him too. Evanna's directions only revealed themselves when he was on foot, so he had to abandon the easy alternatives and walk. But the path wasn't difficult and it was a pleasant time of year. He enjoyed the journey more than any he had undertaken recently.

Finally, months after setting out, he arrived at a small hill in a clearing. There was a cave near the base of the hill and a pond further down. Larten didn't see the mouth of the cave the first time he looked. If he hadn't felt certain that this was the place, he would have walked by. But when he forced himself to peer harder, he saw the cave clearly and made towards it.

There were lots of frogs by the rim of the pond, croaking noisily. Some were oddly coloured and a few had strange, ink-like markings on their heads and backs. Larten decided to investigate further and set out to catch one of the frogs.

"I wouldn't do that," someone said as he crept towards the pond. Larten looked up and spotted a girl no more than twelve or thirteen years old. She was carrying a bucket and staring at him seriously. "They're poisonous."

"Poisonous frogs?" Larten asked dubiously.

"Sacs along their tongues," the girl said. "If they hit your skin, they'll break and poison will seep in. Death within minutes, even if you're a vampire."

"You know what I am?"

The girl nodded. "My Lady has been expecting you." She pulled a face and shook the bucket. "That's why I'm dragging this. Evanna said you'd want a hot bath when you arrived, so I've been fetching water for the last couple of hours."

"My apologies," Larten said. "I can carry that for you if you like."

The girl smiled shyly. "That's all right. I can manage."

They chatted as they walked to the cave. The girl was called Malora. She couldn't remember her surname — Evanna had taken her as an apprentice when she was five or six and much of her early life was a mystery.

"Did your parents let Evanna take you or did they sell you to her?" Larten asked.

"They didn't *sell* me," Malora huffed. "I'm not a slave, even if my Lady treats me like one much of the time."

Larten smiled. "I have heard such tales of woe before. Does Arra Sails still serve here?"

"Never heard of her," Malora said. "Was she one of Evanna's apprentices?"

"Aye. She did not like her mistress any more than you seem to."

"Nobody does," Malora snorted. "She had four other girls when I came. I'm the only one left, and I don't think I'll hang around much longer either. As soon as I find someone to escort me safely back to the normal world, I'm gone!"

Larten chuckled. The girl was young but feisty, like Arra had been. It was a pity she wasn't older — maybe he would have had more success wooing her than he'd had with the fiery Miss Sails.

As they neared the cave, Evanna appeared. She looked exactly as she had the last time he'd seen her. She hadn't changed or aged. Her hair was long and dirty, she still wore ropes, and her nails were cut in the same unusual fashion.

"Welcome, wanderer." She curtsied before Larten, then hugged him hard. She didn't pick him off the ground, but she did pinch his cheek. "I thought you were never going to pay me a visit," she chided him. "Come — the bath is ready."

Larten frowned. "What makes you think I am desperate to have a bath?"

"It's not for you, fool," she snorted. "Don't you remember what you said when we last parted?" He stared at her blankly. "You promised to scrub my back," she reminded him, and as he recalled that brash boast, his face dropped and his cheeks turned several shades redder than they had when she'd pinched him.

Larten spent the next few nights with the Lady of the Wilds, Malora always in close attendance, although the apprentice didn't say much, so he often forgot she was there. The vampire and witch sparred — she enjoyed testing herself in battle against him, although he was sure she could have flattened him with a flick of a wrist if she'd wished — and she treated him to a variety of vegetarian dishes. He had been sceptical of the food at first, but Evanna had surprised him with a variety of extraordinary concoctions. It wasn't enough to sway Larten away from meat, even though she kept urging him to put his carnivorous side behind him, but he wouldn't turn up his nose at vegetables and fruit again.

Evanna had some news of Seba and Wester, which she shared. It was all minor – reports of changes Seba had made in his role as quartermaster, news that Wester was close to becoming a guard – but Larten lapped up the titbits.

In return Larten told Evanna of his indecision. It was good to get the doubts and regrets off his chest, to admit how sorry he felt about the way he'd spoken to Seba, bemoan the years he had wasted and wonder aloud at what the future held. He asked her for advice, but she was reluctant to give any.

"When it comes to the future, I have to be careful," she said. "I have the gift of foresight – I see things that have not yet happened – so I can't interfere."

"Have you seen *my* future?" Larten asked eagerly.

"Parts of it," she said cagily. "I try not to learn too much about the destinies of those I like. It's not nice knowing how much time a friend has left, the hardships they'll face, the pain they'll suffer."

"You see hardship and suffering in my future?" Larten asked quietly.

"I was speaking in general terms," she corrected him. "We all suffer one way or another. In your case..." She seemed set to reveal something and he leant forward eagerly. Then she paused and cocked her head. Larten thought he heard a faint ticking noise – a watch perhaps – but he couldn't place it.

"Destiny watches over all of us," she said softly. "But some catch its eye more than others." She gazed at Malora and her expression was troubled. Then her head swung towards the mouth of the cave. By the way her face creased, Larten thought that somebody must be lurking there. But he could see no one and moments later the witch waved away her worries.

"This is not the time to worry about what the future might bring," she said. "Let us drink and be merry. Your fate will reveal itself in due course, as it always does. But muse on this the next time you fret about your path — we always travel the way we must. You might think that you have strayed, but no one ever steps from the path of destiny. Your doubts have always been waiting for you. Accept them, deal with them, and you will find your way to that which destiny requires of you.

"For better or for worse," she finished glumly and would say no more about it, leaving Larten to puzzle over her strange mutterings for a long time to come.

* * *

That night Larten took Evanna's advice to drink and be merry a little too closely to heart. Ale was his tipple of choice, but he had tried most alcoholic brews in his time. Since Evanna preferred wine, he drank it with her, even though she warned him that it was stronger than the wines he was familiar with.

"I can drink any man under the table," Larten laughed. "And any vampire too."

"What about a sorceress?" Evanna asked.

"I will give it a good try," he winked, toasting her health and asking Malora to refill his glass.

In a light mood, Evanna drank more than usual, and although she could never get drunk – it was physically impossible for one of her kind – she relaxed to the point where she wasn't thinking clearly. She laughed at Larten's jokes and smiled when he flattered her. The flattery was nothing new, but her response was different. Larten began to think that she might be warming to his advances. The more he drank, the surer he became that the Lady of the Wilds was falling for his charms. She would become his mate and they'd have many powerful children. He wouldn't have to worry about his future then — every vampire would idolise him, regardless of whether he'd completed his training or not.

"Evanna," he murmured late in the night. His voice

was only slightly slurred, but inside his head was spinning. "Do you remember the form you took before? The beautiful lady you became?"

"Are you saying I'm not beautiful now?" she snorted.

"Of course you are!" he cried. "You are always a delight to behold. But that other form... you know the one I mean... that was *nice*. Could you change again?"

"Don't be impudent," Evanna snarled, but she was smirking at the same time.

"Please, Lady, I beg you, give me a vision to send me to bed mesmerised and dreamy."

Evanna usually rejected such pleas – she only changed form to suit herself – but Malora saw her mistress smile in an odd way and sensed trouble brewing. The girl topped up the glasses for Evanna and Larten, then slipped away. They thought she was going to bed, but Malora had other plans. If things worked out the way she suspected, this would be an eventful night, not just for the witch and vampire, but for her too.

Evanna didn't notice her apprentice pick up a bag from beside her bed and slip outside. She was still considering Larten's request. Seeing this, he pressed harder.

"It was a most fair form, Lady. Please let me worship before it again."

"Save your worship for the gods," Evanna sniffed, but she decided to oblige him. Her body shimmered and moments later she was slim and tall, her hair long and blonde, her eyes soft and deep. Larten had never heard of a fairy-tale princess more beautiful than this. His heart leapt as it had on that previous occasion and the laughter drained from him.

"This pleases you, young monkey?" Evanna purred, twirling for him, letting the hem of her dress swish around her like a mist.

"It pleases me a lot," Larten said weakly. He'd meant to come out with some lavish compliment, but that was the best he could manage.

"Vampires are simple creatures," Evanna giggled. "So easy to please. I wish I was like you. Life would be so straightforward if I could be content with shining like an angel, winning the heart of every man who saw me. I think I would…"

Evanna kept talking, but Larten was no longer focused on her words. His heart was pounding and he had only one thought in his head. Not even a tiny part of him cried caution. He yearned for Evanna totally, as he had never longed for a woman before.

He rose shakily as Evanna prattled on, steadied

himself, wiped his lips dry, then took hold of the heavenly maiden in the long white dress. Evanna thought he wanted to dance and she laughed. But then he leant forward and kissed her, and everything suddenly, drastically changed.

"You cur!" Evanna yelled, more shocked than outraged. She pulled back from him and he tried to follow. Snarling, she lashed out with her right hand. The long nail on her little finger caught the flesh high up his left cheek, dug in deep and ripped a channel down to the side of his lip, where it tore free.

Larten shrieked and fell backwards, blood oozing from the wound, eyes wide with fright and pain. For a moment he thought Evanna was going to finish him off and he cowered as she fixed him with a glare and her hands rose into claws.

Then the Lady of the Wilds caught herself and took a step back. "Get out!" she barked.

Larten didn't wait to be told a second time. Stumbling to his feet, he ran for his life, trying to stem the flow of blood by tearing a strip of material from his shirt and pressing it to his cheek.

Evanna only meant for him to leave her sight and come back once she'd calmed down. But as he ran, she realised he had taken her order the wrong way. He thought she was banishing him. She started to call after him, to say that he could stay and she would repair the flesh of his face so that he didn't get a scar. But as the words formed on her lips, she heard a soft ticking sound. Her chest tightened and she almost called to him anyway. But she knew that she couldn't. This was destiny and it wasn't her place to interfere in such workings.

"It most certainly isn't," someone said in a pleasant yet chilling voice. "You did well to hold your tongue. I might have had to cut it out if you hadn't."

Evanna saw a pair of green boots coming across the floor towards her. The man inside them must have been standing almost directly in Larten's way when he fled, but she wasn't surprised that the vampire hadn't seen the uninvited guest. The tiny meddler only revealed himself when he wanted to be noticed, and only when such sightings were guaranteed to lead to conflict and mayhem.

"I didn't know that you were watching him," Evanna said softly.

"Oh, yes," her visitor smirked. "I have been keeping a close eye on Master Crepsley for a long time now. He's heading down a deliciously dangerous path and I plan to be there when he comes to the drop at the end. In his darkest hour I will be at hand to reach out to him and offer him hope. What a lucky man he is to have a friend such as myself watching out for him. Don't you agree, daughter?"

Closing her eyes, Evanna sighed and offered up a short prayer for Larten and Malora, even though she knew, as an agent of destiny with the power of foresight, that her prayer wouldn't help the poor, doomed pair in the slightest.

CHAPTER EIGHTEEN

Larten staggered down the hill from the cave, his cheek stinging, blood dripping from the sodden rag covering his wound. The pain and night air sobered him up briskly. How could he have been such a fool? Evanna had killed vampires for less. He didn't blame her for cutting his cheek. He was just surprised he'd got out of the cave alive. In a way he was sorry that he had — at least he wouldn't have had to live with his shame if she'd killed him.

On unsteady legs he weaved his way to the edge of the pond. Making sure he wasn't in range of any poisonous frogs, he knelt and peeled the rag from his cheek. Fresh blood cascaded down his chin. Moaning softly – more from guilt than pain – he cupped a handful of water and splashed it over his face. It stung, but not as much as he'd thought it would.

Lowering his head, he drove it deep beneath the water and held it there until he ran out of breath.

When he came up gasping, he heard footsteps. He guessed that the witch had come after him. Instead of fleeing, he held his position, staring into the water as the ripples cleared, hoping to die honourably when she attacked.

But when he glimpsed her reflection as the person came closer, he realised it wasn't Evanna. It was her apprentice, Malora.

"Does it hurt terribly?" she asked, kneeling beside him.

"I have known worse," Larten sighed. He had suffered many more serious injuries while training inside Vampire Mountain. But his pride had only taken this severe a beating on that initial night of fighting at his first Council.

Malora passed him a clean handkerchief. He thanked her with a short smile, then winced as he pressed it to his wound. "I have a needle and thread," she said, patting a bag by her knees. "I can stitch you up if you wish. If I sew cleanly, the scar shouldn't be too noticeable."

Larten considered her offer, then dismissed it. "I will bear the scar openly," he said. "It will remind me what a fool I was and hopefully help me never repeat the mistake that I made tonight."

Malora smirked. "You tried to kiss her, didn't you?"

Larten nodded. "She struck me, then chased me off. I am shocked that she did not kill me."

"It was the wine. If you'd been sober, I'd be wrapping your severed head in a cloth now. You're not the first to try and take advantage of her," Malora said in answer to his raised eyebrow. "I've had to pick up the pieces of a couple of overly amorous suitors in the past. But Evanna knows the effect wine has on mortals. You angered her, obviously, but she realised your pass was more clumsy and innocent than cynical and insulting."

"Will you give her my apologies in the morning?" Larten asked.

"No," Malora surprised him. "I'm leaving with you."

"What are you talking about?" Larten frowned and the gesture brought a fresh torrent of blood from the cut.

"I told you I was unhappy," Malora said. "I've been waiting for an escort to lead me out of here. You'll do."

"Wait a minute," Larten said, alarmed. "I am no escort. You do not know where I am going. I might not see another human for months."

She shrugged. "That doesn't bother me. I might not even go back to my human life. I'm interested in vampires. I want to learn about your ways, maybe become one of you."

"No!" Larten barked. "I do not want an assistant. I

am not a General. You heard me talking with Evanna. I am confused, lost. I do not know what I want for myself, so I can hardly make decisions for *you*."

"I'm not asking you to make any decisions for me," Malora said coolly. "I've already made them. I'm coming with you. Where you lead doesn't matter. I don't care that you're not part of the clan, that you might never be again. I just want to travel with you a while. When I've had enough of your company, I'll move on."

Larten stared at the girl, not sure what to say. "You are too young," he tried. "A vampire's life is hard and testing. I could not make allowances for a child."

"If I'm old enough to be a witch's apprentice, I'm old enough to serve a vampire," Malora huffed. "As for making allowances, that won't be a problem. I need your help to get out of here, but once we reach civilisation I'll look after myself. If I can't keep up, you have my permission to cut me loose."

Larten tried one last tactic. "You might not be safe travelling with me," he said darkly. "What if I try to kiss you like I kissed Evanna?"

"Nonsense," Malora snorted. "You're not the type of man to make an advance on a girl like me. Even if you were… well, I have sharp nails too, only I'd slit your throat, not your cheek."

Larten laughed, then grimaced as his wound flared. "Very well," he muttered. "As long as you understand that you are not my assistant, just a companion, aye?"

"Of course," Malora said meekly, then added wickedly, "*master*."

Larten pushed himself up. He offered Malora a hand, but she waved it aside and hopped to her feet. Smiling brightly, she asked, "Which way?"

Larten blinked, then looked around and pointed to his right.

Malora shook her head.

"Left?" he tried weakly.

"An excellent choice," she beamed and started down the path ahead of him. Larten thought about fleeing in the opposite direction – she couldn't catch him if he flitted – but he didn't want to leave the girl alone in the dark. Wringing blood from the handkerchief, he reapplied it to his cheek, rolled his eyes at the heavens, then followed after Malora like a lamb.

PART FIVE

"And like a sliver of deadly mercury, he attacked."

CHAPTER NINETEEN

Larten blew his nose, doubled over and coughed. His face was red when he came up for air and he had to spit a mouthful of thick, horrible phlegm into an already laden handkerchief.

"Give me that," Malora said, taking the snot-riddled rag and handing him a fresh replacement. Her nose wrinkled as she dropped the handkerchief into a tub of hot water. This was the fifth he'd got through since sunset.

"I didn't think vampires could catch the flu," Malora muttered.

"It is rare," Larten groaned. "We are immune to most sicknesses. But when the strain of vampire flu strikes, it strikes hard."

He shivered and pulled his blanket tighter around himself, even though it did no good. He had come down with the symptoms a couple of weeks ago. He'd worsened steadily for ten nights, but then seemed to recover. He was surprised by his rapid comeback — vampire flu often killed those it struck, or stayed in their system for months on end.

Malora pressed the back of her hand to the vampire's forehead, checking his temperature. She hadn't learnt much in her years with Evanna, but she'd picked up some helpful healing tips.

"Drink more broth," she grunted.

"What about ale?" Larten asked hopefully.

"If I catch you anywhere near a mug of ale, you'll be sleeping in the street," she snapped. It was a familiar threat and he knew better than to dismiss it lightly. She had driven him from his room more than once in the past when he'd drunk too much and irritated her.

Larten blew his nose again and studied Malora over the top of his handkerchief. She had grown into a beautiful young woman. She kept her hair short and wore trousers more often than skirts, since they were easier to travel in, but nobody could have mistaken her for a boy. She caught the eye of gentlemen wherever they went. But even though she'd celebrated her sixteenth birthday earlier in the year – an age at which, in Larten's youth, many girls had already married and given birth – she had never shown any interest in the men who wished to woo her.

"Are there no spells you could use to clear this up?" Larten asked.

"Evanna probably knows a few," Malora said with fake sincerity. "We could visit her if you like."

Larten blanched and his fingers went automatically to his scar, which he traced from top to bottom. The prominent scar would have been considered disfiguring by humans, but he carried it with pride. It reminded him of his foolishness, but also his daring and good fortune — there were few vampires who could say they had invoked the wrath of the Lady of the Wilds and lived to tell the tale.

He shuffled to the window and stared at the street outside. There weren't many lamps, but he could see clearly, albeit through watery eyes. He wasn't sure where they were staying. Malora had guided him for the last fortnight. They usually slept in crypts or caves, but she had insisted on inns while he was sick. He'd resisted at first – he thought clear air would be better for him – but he was so poorly by the third night that he would have slept on top of a giant needle if she'd ordered it.

As he was staring out of the window, he saw an elderly gentleman approach. The man had long, white hair and a flowing, silver beard. His right ear had been cut off long ago and his face was lined with wrinkles. Although he looked ancient, and was even older than he appeared, he walked with a spring in his step that many younger men lacked.

"I do not believe it," Larten gasped. "Paris Skyle!"

"The Prince?" Malora asked.

"Aye. You know him?"

"Only by reputation." She stuck out an arm as an excited Larten tried to dart past her. "Where do you think you're going?"

"To catch him," Larten said impatiently. "I have not seen Paris in ages. I must stop him before he—"

"It *could* be coincidence that of all the inns in the world, he happens to pass by this one," Malora said witheringly. "But what are the odds of that?"

"You think he has come to see me?" Larten asked, delight giving way to nervousness.

"Have another look — has he moved on or is he coming in?"

Larten returned to the window and watched as Paris paused, studied the sign outside the inn, then entered.

"You are as canny as Evanna," he muttered.

"Nowhere near," Malora sniffed. "But even the dumbest woman has more sense than the average man. Wait!" she shouted as Larten tried to push past her again.

"What now?" he scowled.

"You're not meeting a Prince dressed like that," she said firmly. He hadn't changed his clothes recently. They were filthy and smelly, spattered with dry – and some fresh – flecks of spit and snot.

"Paris is a *vampire* Prince," Larten said. "They do not care about looks."

"Be that as it may, I'm not letting you leave in such a state. I'm going to call for a hot bath. Once you've bathed, dressed in clean clothes and blown your nose a few more times, you can present yourself to him."

"But if he is waiting for me—" Larten exploded.

"–he will have to be patient," Malora finished calmly. "I'll take him a glass of wine to keep him quiet – they don't have a great selection here, but there are a few nice bottles tucked away in the back – and say that you'll be with him presently."

"How do you know what wine they have?" Larten asked as she let herself out.

"I'm your assistant," Malora said. "It's my job to know things like that. Now make sure you're undressed by the time I get back, and don't be shy, you've nothing I haven't seen before."

"*Malora!*" Larten gasped, but she was already gone.

Paris was amused and impressed by Malora, and when Larten was finally allowed to present himself to his elderly friend, they spent the early part of the night discussing her. He told the Prince how they'd met and grinned sheepishly as Paris howled with laughter when he heard how Larten had acquired his scar.

"Don't tell anyone else that story," Paris chuckled. "Let them think you got it fighting a lion or a vampaneze."

"Evanna is far more dangerous than that," Larten said.

"Aye, but she's still a woman. Trust me, if you want to keep your reputation, be mysterious about this."

"I did not think that I had a reputation," Larten said glumly.

"In some quarters you do," Paris replied kindly. "You're not the first vampire to lose his way. We understand how difficult it can be to choose the path of the Generals. If you return to the fold, you'll find us more welcoming than you imagine. We'll even accept your strange choice of assistant."

"Malora is not a real assistant," Larten said. "She does not show any interest in being blooded. I think she just likes having someone to boss around."

"Show me a woman who doesn't," Paris chortled and called for another glass of the interesting wine that Malora had found for them.

The pair chatted the night away, retiring to a cosy back-room when all the other customers had gone to bed, where they drank by the light of a single fat candle. Paris sipped wine and Larten quaffed ale. (He would get into trouble for defying Malora, but he didn't care. This was an occasion for ale.) Paris relayed the latest news from Vampire Mountain. Seba and Wester were well. Wester had become a guard and was proud as a peacock.

"Seba is just as proud," Paris said.

Larten was too, though it reminded him of his own failures and he had to strain to keep his smile in place.

Paris gave Larten some advice on the best way to fight off the flu. The Prince had endured a few bad cases himself over the centuries and he recommended herbs that were no longer fashionable but which had eased the worst of his suffering in the past.

"But to be honest, you just have to ride it out as best you can," he added. "It will plague you for at least another month. It comes and goes in waves, so don't think you've beaten it. Wrap up warm, heed Malora's advice, and pray to the gods to let you live if that's their will."

Shortly before dawn, when they both had a rosy glow from the wine and ale, Paris spoke of his real reason for tracking down the stray vampire.

"Seba is in poor spirits," he said.

"Sick?" Larten yelped with alarm.

"No — upset. He misses you, but there's more to it than that. Seba doesn't care whether or not you become a General, live among humans or take some other path. He just wants you to be happy. But from reports he's received over the years, you're not. He senses you struggling and wandering blindly. That troubles him."

"I never wanted to disappoint Seba," Larten said miserably. "I wanted him to be proud of me, like he is of Wester."

"Then give him something to be proud of," Paris said softly but pointedly. "In the name of the gods, Larten, *choose*. You're not a new-blood. You've enjoyed your wild years and had time to reflect since distancing yourself from the clan. Surely by now you must have some idea of what you want to do with your life."

Larten sighed. "It is complicated. I yearn to be a General, but I feel there is more I must do before I return and complete my training. I do not know what, but at the moment the thought of coming back..." He shook his head.

"What if you could train outside of Vampire Mountain?" Paris asked. "I could be your tutor and teach you as we travel."

Larten was stunned by the offer. Seba had said that the Princes were interested in him, but he hadn't believed it — he'd thought his old master was merely trying to flatter him. This was an amazing opportunity. Only a fool would turn it down. The chance to train under a Prince would probably never come his way again. And yet...

For some reason Larten recalled the ticking sound he'd heard in Evanna's cave. That noise disturbed his dreams occasionally, though he had no idea why, just as he didn't know why he should think of it now.

"Sleep on it," Paris said, seeing the flicker of temptation in Larten's bloodshot eyes. He rose and stretched. "There's no rush. I don't have to leave for a few more nights. Think it over. Discuss it with Malora. I won't press you for an answer."

"You are too good to me, Sire," Larten mumbled, bowing his head respectfully.

"I know," Paris laughed then went upstairs to the room that Malora had prepared for him, where he was stunned to find a coffin lying on a couple of tables. "Now this is what I call first-class service," he murmured as he lay inside and happily pulled the lid closed over himself.

CHAPTER TWENTY

As soon as Larten rose in the afternoon, Malora scolded him for drinking the night before. He tried to defend his actions and said he thought the ale had done him some good, but she made him take a cold bath to purge himself of the evils of alcohol. Afterwards he told her of Paris's offer and asked her opinion. She thought about it a long time before answering.

"It's not a question of *if* you become a General but *when*."

Larten was surprised by her certainty. "You think so?"

"You were born to be a General. It's just a matter of whether you think this is the right time to complete your training or if you'd rather roam the world a few more years, moping about what a hard choice you have to face."

"That is a cruel way to put it," Larten muttered.

"But true," she smirked. "I don't know why you've

strayed for so long. I doubt you even know that yourself. If you feel this is the wrong time to commit, say no to Paris. But you should consider the possibility that the *right* time might never come. Maybe you'll feel indecisive all your life and you just have to pick a moment to say, *I am going to become a General, damn the consequences*." She did an accurate impression of him and he found himself smiling.

"What about you?" Larten asked. "If I return to the clan, you will have to study hard before I can blood you."

"Don't be ridiculous," Malora snorted. "I've no intention of letting you blood me. Vampirism doesn't interest me in the slightest."

Larten gawped at her. "Then why, by the black blood of Harnon Oan, have you been following me around the world?" he thundered.

"You really thought I wanted to become a vampire?" she asked. When he nodded, she sighed. "I knew you were naive, but I didn't think you were *that* dense." As he puffed himself up to bellow at her, she reached out and gently caressed his scar. Her touch calmed him.

"I never wanted to join the clan," Malora said softly. "I said I did because that was what you needed to hear. I don't care about returning to the human world either. I only want to be with you for all the nights and days that I have left. I knew you were the man for me the moment I saw you."

"Wait a minute!" Larten gulped. He hadn't been expecting a declaration of love. "You're a child," he wheezed.

"A young lady," she corrected him. "And getting older. I'm patient. I can wait until you decide I'm old enough."

"But—"

"If you're about to say that I'll always be a girl in your eyes," she interrupted sharply, "*don't*. You might reject me, but don't insult me. I won't stand for that, not from any man, even the love of my life."

"The love of…" Larten echoed weakly.

"You don't need to do anything now," Malora said sweetly. "You're slow, like most men, but you'll catch up soon and realise you love me as much as I love you. I just want you to know that, in the meantime, I'll follow you no matter where you go. Your path is mine because my heart is yours.

"Now go enjoy yourself with Paris. I'll be waiting for you when you get back. I'll always wait for you, my love."

With that she shooed him out of the room and left him to stare at the closed door in bewilderment. After he'd scratched his head for the sixth time, he turned and trudged down the steps to get a drink and mull things over.

Paris was nowhere to be found — Larten assumed the elderly Prince was still asleep — but a middle-aged man with a beard was sitting at one of the tables, writing in a notebook. He hailed Larten and invited him over. As Larten cautiously sat, the man said, "You're Master Skyle's friend, aren't you?"

Larten relaxed. "You know Paris?"

"Oh, yes," the man beamed. "My name's Abraham, but please call me Bram."

Larten gave his own name, shook hands and accepted the mug of ale he was offered.

"What are you writing?" Larten asked.

"Just a few ideas for a story I'm researching."

"You write stories?" Larten was interested. He had met several authors over the decades and found them a curious bunch.

"Novels, mostly. You might have heard of *The Snake's Pass*, perhaps?"

Larten shook his head. "I am not a reader. I never learnt." He expected the man to look surprised, maybe even sneer at him, but Bram only shrugged.

"You might be better off. Writing is my life — on top of running a theatre — but I often think I'd have been more successful and a lot happier if I'd never taken up a pen. The muse is a cruel mistress."

Larten pressed Bram for details of his books and the theatre. He learnt that the writer was from Ireland but now lived in London, "when I'm not trotting around Europe trying to finish this dratted novel!"

When Larten asked about his new book, Bram waved aside the question. "I never discuss a work in progress. I don't want to jinx myself. Tell me about your life instead. You're a vampire like Paris, aren't you?"

"A vampire, aye, but hardly like Paris," Larten chuckled.

"He's something of a legend, isn't he?" Bram smiled.

"Among vampires, certainly," Larten agreed. Over the next few hours he told Bram some of his favourite Paris Skyle stories, becoming more eloquent the more he drank. After a while Bram asked if he could take notes, "just for fun," and Larten said that of course he could.

Bram was interested in the rest of the clan, as well as the vampaneze. He wanted to know when vampires had stopped killing when they fed, and if any ever overstepped the mark now.

"Never," Larten said. "The punishment is severe if you break that law."

"A stake through the heart?" Bram guessed.

"Or something similarly fatal," Larten nodded.

"The stake tradition started with Vlad, I suppose," Bram murmured, trying to disguise his interest in the answer.

"Vlad?" Larten blinked.

"Vlad the Impaler? Also known as Vlad Tepes or Vlad Dracula? He was one of the clan, wasn't he?"

"No, you interfering busybody," somebody growled behind them. "He was not."

Larten stared up at a glowering Paris Skyle, who had appeared behind Bram's chair. Bram choked back a gulp and turned, smiling shakily. "Good evening, Paris, I'm glad to see—"

"What have you been telling this *scribe?*" Paris snarled.

"Nothing much," Larten said hesitantly, beginning to realise that he had been speaking freely with someone he didn't know. "He asked about you and the clan."

"And you told him what he wanted to hear?" Paris snapped.

Larten flushed. "Yes. I was open with him. He said that he knew you and I did not think I needed to be wary in his company."

"Think a bit harder next time," Paris said coldly, then placed a hand on Bram's shoulder and squeezed. Bram winced, but didn't try to escape. "You're persistent, Master Stoker. I assume *you* sent me the message requesting my presence across town. You wanted my friend to yourself for a while, aye?"

"I need more facts for my story," Bram said quietly.

"*Facts?* I thought it was going to be a work of fiction."

"It is. I gave you my word that I wouldn't do anything to expose or harm the clan. But the more I know about you, the more steps I can take to ensure I don't write something that accidentally leads people to investigate your movements."

"If you didn't write about us at all, you could be even surer," Paris said icily.

"Someone's going to write about vampires sooner or later," Bram said. "Would you prefer a work of fiction, where I blur the truth and give the world something fantastical, or a tome that mentions Vampire Mountain, Generals and the rest?"

Paris thought about that, then removed his hand. "Perhaps you're correct. If your story tricks people into thinking that vampires are mythical beasts, it may do some good. Not that I think many will read it — people want uplifting tales, not morbid stories of bloodsucking creatures of the night."

"You might be surprised," Bram said, picking up his pen again. "You'll answer my questions?"

"Aye," Paris nodded, "but not tonight. I'm entertaining a friend. Remain a few nights and I will let you have your... how did you put it last time... your interview with a vampire."

"Can we shake on that?" Bram asked, extending a hand.

"No," Paris said flatly. "A vampire doesn't need to shake hands once he has given his word. Go from here, Abraham Stoker, and give me the space I asked for. I will speak with you shortly."

Bram nodded and gathered his belongings. "Sorry if I got you into trouble," he said to Larten.

"Move along," Paris barked. "We haven't dined yet and that neck of yours looks ripe for the biting."

Bram flashed Paris a dark look, then backed away from the table, tossed some coins to the innkeeper and let himself out. Paris watched him leave, then sat and called for a glass of wine.

"Sire, I'm sorry if I—" Larten began.

"It matters not," Paris said curtly. "That man has been dogging my footsteps for three years. He would have forced a confrontation eventually. I'm not worried. I'm sure his book won't amount to much even if it's published, which I doubt. Let us speak of more important issues. Have you considered what we spoke of?"

Larten nodded.

"And?"

If Paris had asked the question a few hours earlier, Larten would have accepted the Prince's offer to train him. But his careless conversation with Bram Stoker had disturbed him. Paris had made light of it, but Larten knew he should have been more circumspect. Even new-bloods didn't discuss the clan with anyone they couldn't trust completely. Larten's self-confidence had been shaken. He could have taken more time to answer – Paris wasn't rushing him – but his head was sore from the flu, which seemed to be returning with a vengeance, and the ale was sitting heavily in his stomach. All he wanted was to slink back to his room to brood.

"I thank you for offering to take me under your wing, but I do not think that I am ready to resume my lessons," he said.

Paris sighed. "I had hoped for a different answer."

"I am sorry to disappoint you, Sire. I mean no disrespect."

"You must do as your heart dictates, of course, but..." Paris hesitated then pressed on. "Wander if you must, Larten, but the longer you live in exile, the more risks you run."

"Risks, Sire?" Larten frowned.

"You risk losing yourself forever," Paris said. "You might never find your path, and end up becoming something bitter and adrift. This world can corrupt a lone vampire. We are beings of the night, but the darkness is a dangerous place for one without friends."

"I have Malora," Larten said softly.

"She might face even worse dangers," Paris retorted, then grimaced. "But I'm doing what I said I wouldn't, trying to persuade you. Ignore my last comments. I am old and addled. Like all old men, I see pitfalls where none exist. You are eager to return to your room, I know, but pray have one last drink with me. I promise not to speak of this matter again."

Larten had a final drink with Paris, but he couldn't enjoy it. He kept thinking about what the Prince had said. Talk of dangers in the darkness had unsettled him. He had survived this long by himself and never felt under threat. And no harm could befall Malora while she had Larten to protect her. Yet he sensed truth – almost a prediction – in Paris's warning.

Coughing heavily, wiping phlegm from his lips with one of the handkerchiefs which Malora had washed clean for him that morning, Larten struggled to pinpoint the source of his unease, but he couldn't. He decided in the end that the flu had simply sapped him of his strength. That was why he felt so gloomy. It would pass when he got better. Everything would be fine then, he was sure of it. After all, in this world of humans, he was little better than a monster, and what did a monster have to be afraid of in the dark?

CHAPTER
TWENTY-ONE

"Going to sea!" Larten snarled, dragging himself towards the docks.

"This is a bad idea," Malora gasped, trying to tug him back, but having as much luck as a dog would have with an elephant.

"Want to sail... the seven seas." Larten laughed. "Sick of these towns and... cities. Got to keep... going. Don't trust land."

He stopped in the middle of a street and glared at the people who were looking at him oddly. He was dressed in a smart pair of trousers and a dirty white jumper which he'd bought from a sailor the night before, with a shoe on his right foot and an old boot on his left. He was holding a lady's umbrella over his head to protect him from the sun.

Malora thought that the jumper had put the idea into his head. The flu was ultimately to blame – it had ebbed and flared in him over the last six weeks, and was now worse than ever — but he'd been content to stay inside and follow her lead until he bought that stupid jumper. As soon as he pulled it on, he began ranting about going to sea — he had smelled the salt air a couple of nights before when they'd come to this town. She'd managed to calm him and get him to sleep, but he had woken with the notion fresh in his head. Without pausing to eat, he had dressed and hobbled down to the docks, Malora hurrying to keep up, trying to make him change his mind.

"Larten!" she snapped as he stared around. "This isn't a good idea. We'll go on a long cruise when you feel better. You're sick. We should stay somewhere warm and dry, so that you can—"

"No!" he bellowed, taking off again. "Vampire hunters on land. They'll stick a stake through… my heart. Have to get to sea. Life on the waves. Aye!"

Malora argued with him all the way, but he ignored her. At the docks he strode around like a madman, checking all the ships. He stopped several sailors and asked if they knew which boat was making the longest journey. Some shrugged him off and didn't answer. Those who responded gave conflicting reports. But when a third man mentioned the *Pearly Tornado*, Larten's mind was decided.

Malora was almost crying. When Larten found the

gangplank, she darted ahead of him and set herself in his way. "No further," she croaked. "This is madness. If you go on, you'll go without me. I'll leave you here, Larten, I swear I will."

"Then leave," he said coldly and leapt over her. As he stormed up the plank, Malora cursed, looked longingly at the dry land of the docks, then followed him. She tried to put on a brave face – "Very well. I've always wanted to see more of the world." – but she was dreadfully worried. The flu was playing havoc with Larten. If it worsened at sea, he was a dead man.

A boy was swabbing the deck when Larten boarded. The boy glanced at the shoddily dressed stranger, shrugged and spat on the boards, then wiped them clean.

"You!" Larten yelled. "Where's your captain?"

"In his cabin," the boy said.

"Get him for me."

The boy was going to tell the man to run his own errands, but then he spotted Malora and straightened. "Afternoon, ma'am," he saluted, smiling in what he hoped was a rakish way. "Can I help ye at all?"

"Larten," Malora tried one last time, but he shook his head aggressively. She gave up and sighed. "I am Malora. This is my master, Larten Crepsley. He seeks travel on board this ship."

"This ain't a passenger ship, ma'am," the boy said. "We sometimes take a few paying customers when there's space, but mostly it's crew and cargo. I don't think there's any cabins left on this trip."

"Did you hear that?" Malora said brightly.

"Nonsense," Larten sniffed, tossing a coin to the boy. He caught it midair and pocketed it immediately. "What is your name?"

"Daniel Abrams," the boy said smartly.

"You will get another coin when you bring your captain to me."

"Yes, sir, Master Crepsley, sir!" Daniel yapped then raced off.

The captain was a gruff, thickset man. He eyed Larten dubiously, but like Daniel, his face lit up when he spotted the pretty Malora. "Sir. Ma'am. Can I be of help?"

"We seek a cabin," Larten said.

"Alas, this isn't a passenger ship. We have a handful o' passengers, but we've already squeezed in as many as we can fer this journey. If it's America ye're looking fer, I can recommend—"

"I do not care where you are going," Larten snapped, then paused. "America?"

"Ultimately," the captain nodded. "Got a few stops t' make first, and we're going by way o' Greenland, but—"

Chapter Twenty-one

"Greenland!" Larten yelled with excitement. "That is where I want to go."

"A strange place t' want t' get off, sir," the captain said. "But I can recommend a couple o' ships fer there too."

"I do not want any other ship," Larten growled. "This is the ship for me. The *Pearly Tornado* — a fine name, a fine ship and a fine captain."

"Very nice o' ye t' say, sir, but I'm afraid I really can't—"

Larten dug into his pockets, pulled out all of his money and thrust it at the astonished captain. "Is that enough? Malora, give him more if he wants."

"I don't think he needs any more," Malora said quietly. She shared a look with the captain and took back a couple of notes. He didn't object — in fact he seemed relieved. "Will that cover the cost of our voyage and help you persuade some of your other passengers to make way for us?"

"It will," the captain said weakly. "But ye'll have t' share a cabin."

"No," Malora said firmly. "We need a cabin of our own."

"But—" the captain began to protest. Malora handed him one of the notes she had retrieved and the captain glumly pocketed the money. "Give me fifteen minutes. I'll have it sorted fer ye by then."

"And captain," Malora called him back. "Fresh linen, if you please."

He grinned thinly and tipped his hat to her. "Aye, ma'am."

The *Pearly Tornado* set sail on the next tide. Larten missed the launch. He was asleep in their cabin, tossing and turning from the fever. Malora had washed him down once already, after he had vomited all over himself and the sheets. The next few days or weeks were going to be hard, until the flu passed. (*Or until he dies*, part of her whispered, but she preferred not to consider that grim possibility.)

When she felt the ship get under way, Malora left Larten and went on deck. This was her first time sailing and she was fascinated by all of the activity going on around her. She had never guessed that the running of a ship would be such a complex process.

The other passengers were on deck too, looking at the shore with sad longing as they pulled away. There were four men, two women and a baby that clung to its mother and cried shrilly. Malora assumed they were going to start a new life in America, and were so poor that they hadn't been able to afford passage on any of the regular ships.

Daniel Abrams – the boy who'd first greeted them – edged up to Malora, spat over the railing and nodded pleasantly. "Yer master's asleep?" he guessed.

"Resting," Malora said.

"He looked right sick when he came aboard," Daniel noted.

"Influenza," Malora said. "He's over the worst of it, but will probably lay low for most of the journey. His eyes are weak from the illness. He can't bear to be out in the sun at the moment — that's why he had the umbrella."

"Ah." Daniel nodded again, this time like a doctor. "If ye need anything, liquor, medicine or hot food, let me know. We don't have much, but I can fetch the best of what there is… fer a price." He coughed uncomfortably, unaccustomed to such bargaining.

Malora smiled at the boy. "My master is a generous man. You will be well rewarded for any services rendered. And you already have my gratitude for making such a kind offer."

Daniel blushed. "Anything ye want, ma'am, just ask fer Master Abrams. I'm a right little jackdaw, me."

Malora remained on deck a couple of hours, adjusting to the swell of the waves, breathing deeply of the salty air. Before returning to her cabin, she asked Daniel to arrange some supplies for them: drink, food and a burner — she said she would cook in their cabin while her master was sick. As he was doing that, she went to check on Larten.

The vampire was awake but poorly. He didn't recognise Malora when she came in — he thought it was Evanna, come to scar the other side of his face. He tried to hide beneath his blankets, but as she whispered his name over and over, his eyes half cleared and he sat up.

"Malora?" he whined.

"Who else?"

"Where are we?"

"On a ship." When he stared at her, she said, "You wanted to see Greenland."

He tried to work out why he might have said such a thing, but his head hurt when he thought too much. "I'm hungry," he whimpered instead.

"Food is on its way."

"No," he said. "The other kind of hunger."

Malora frowned. She had already considered this – it was one of the reasons she hadn't wanted to set sail in the first place – but hadn't thought he'd need to feed so soon.

"Can you wait?" she asked. "We dock at our first port in less than a week. We can slip ashore then and…"

He was already shaking his head. "Can't," he wheezed. "The hunger... I have to feed when it comes. Dangerous not to. Might drink recklessly if I do not sip regularly."

"Very well," she sighed and sat beside him. She rolled up a sleeve, took a knife from her belt and made a small cut beneath her elbow. She didn't wince as the blade bit into her flesh — it would take more than that to make her cry. "Not too much," she murmured as Larten leant forward eagerly. "We have to make it last."

He nodded, then fixed his lips around the cut. Malora smiled and stroked his hair as he fed, her expression and gestures very much like the mother's on deck had been as she'd tried to soothe her wailing baby.

CHAPTER
TWENTY-TWO

Malora hoped that Larten would disembark when they docked. His condition was worsening and he needed rest and warmth. But he wouldn't hear of it. When the fever made him feisty, he insisted on going to Greenland to search for the palace of Perta Vin-Grahl. (Malora had no idea who that was.) In his lower moments he moaned that he wanted to die onboard and be buried at sea. Either way, he had no intention of setting foot ashore at any of their early stops.

Malora never lost her temper, even when he was at his most pitiful and demanding. This was the man she had chosen and she loved him as completely as any sixteen-year-old had ever loved. Nothing he did tested her patience, whether he yelled abuse, wept and asked her to kill him, threw up over her or spat in her face. It was the flu that made him do these things and she refused to blame him for his addle-headed actions.

The captain, Daniel and the rest of the crew were

enamoured with Malora. She spent a lot of time making friends, joking with the sailors, stitching clothes for them, helping out in the kitchen. Daniel was especially fond of her, even though he knew he couldn't win her heart, being younger than her and just starting out in life. He trailed her like a faithful dog whenever he could. He even asked her to teach him how to cook, so that he could spend more time with her in the kitchen. He was a terrible chef, but he stuck with it to be close to Malora.

Because they liked the girl so much, they said nothing critical of her bedridden master. When he roared abusively, they turned a deaf ear to his insults. On the rare occasions when he staggered out of his cabin and caused a disturbance on deck, they veered round him and waited for Malora to usher him back inside. They would have put ashore any other passenger who proved so disruptive, no matter how much he had paid, but for Malora's sake they tolerated the orange-haired nuisance.

Looking after Larten was exhausting, but Malora was equal to the challenge. She worked hard, guarded him fiercely, and let him feed from her when he needed blood. The only problem was that her blood was not going to be enough. He was drinking more than usual because of the fever and she would not be able to supply him indefinitely from her own veins.

When they made their final dock before embarking on the long, uninterrupted stretch to Greenland, Malora tried convincing him to come ashore with her, to feed on another person's blood and restock the vials he carried in case of emergencies. But Larten thought she was trying to trick him, that the ship would sail without them if he got off, so he refused to budge.

Out of desperation, Malora took the vials and went ashore by herself. Scouring dark, unpleasant alleys, she found a number of sailors sleeping off hangovers. Taking care not to hurt them, she made small cuts on their arms and legs and tried to fill the vials. It was a messy job, but she returned with something to show for her efforts, pleased with what she had brought back.

Malora would have been far less pleased if she had spotted Daniel Abrams trailing her through the alleys from one victim to another.

The boy hadn't set out to spy. At first he'd followed after her like he did on ship, simply wanting to be close to the girl. When she started exploring the alleys, he figured he should watch out for her in case she ran into trouble — he had vague notions of saving her life and winning her heart. But when he saw her bleeding the snoring sailors...

Daniel was deeply troubled when he returned. His first instinct was to report it, but he was certain the captain would throw them off if he knew what the sweet-looking girl had been up to. Daniel couldn't care less about Larten Crepsley, but he would miss Malora. In the end he kept his own counsel, but decided to monitor the girl and her mysterious master. He wasn't sure what Malora wanted with the blood. It might have been for some strange medical purpose. But he thought there was something more diabolical going on. He wasn't sure what, but he was certain he'd find out. Daniel was sharp. He would uncover their dark, crimson secret in the end, no matter what it was.

The ship sailed on, one day blurring into another. The waters were calm for that time of year, but they still had to endure a few rough nights when Malora was sure the vessel would capsize. The other passengers were as scared as she was on those occasions, but the crew never looked worried. Malora didn't know if that was because they felt safe, or because as sailors they'd accepted the fact that they were going to die at sea eventually. She never asked — it was better not knowing, in case the answer was the latter.

Larten's spirits improved temporarily, then

darkened again. She had never known a fever like this. She was sure it couldn't be natural, even in a vampire. Paris Skyle could have told her otherwise, and there were herbs and treatments he could have recommended. But as the Prince had tried to tell Larten in the inn, there was only so much a human could understand about the creatures of the night. Larten had cut himself off from the clan and Malora had to deal with the crisis as best she could.

She changed his clothes regularly, bathed him, wiped sweat from his face when the shakes took hold. She made sure he ate and drank enough, and kept the small window open to let in fresh air. He had stopped asking for blood, and though she forced a few drips into his mouth – from another of her cuts, having long since worked through the vials – he spat out most of it. She wasn't sure if he was trying to die or just couldn't digest blood in his weakened condition.

Larten looked like a man on the verge of death. He had aged several years. His skin was saggy and grey, his nails broke off easily, his eyes were red and lifeless. Only his orange hair looked the same as ever — Traz would have been proud to note that his dye could withstand even the ravages of vampire flu.

The last couple of days and nights had been particularly difficult. Larten had thrashed and moaned nonstop, denying Malora sleep. She'd been awake for sixty hours. This was the closest she had come to breaking, but even at her weakest, exhausted and irritable, she kept her wits about her and saw to Larten's needs before her own.

"He'd better appreciate this when he pulls through," she grumbled, refusing to consider the likelihood that he might not recover. "I'll expect presents, fine meals and the grandest hotels. I won't settle for Greenland. He can forget about his palace of ice. I'll insist he treat me to the best New York has to offer."

Malora had heard much about the marvels of New York, mostly from Daniel — he'd never been there, but had picked up tales from other sailors. As Larten snored and lay peacefully for a change – he seemed to be recovering from his latest setback – she thought of the famous city, the delights it could offer, shops full of incredible trinkets and dresses, bustling streets, bright lights that lit up the sky at night. Smiling at the prospect of being able to relax in such a wonderland, she nodded off and was soundly asleep when Larten stirred, rose from his bed and let himself out, moving like a man in a trance.

Screams woke Malora. For a moment she thought it was a nightmare – she'd had plenty of those recently

— but then her head cleared and she realised the screams were real.

Malora grabbed the covers on the bed and whipped them away — no sign of Larten. They were in trouble. She knew it instantly. It was now simply a case of if she could fix the situation before it got any worse.

She hurried out of their cabin and tracked the screams. They were coming from a cabin lower than theirs, where the other passengers were staying. The women were shrieking and the men were shouting. When Malora arrived, some of the crew were already there, gathered around the open door, staring at something inside.

Malora pushed her way through, knowing what she'd find, trying to think of a way to make light of it, to dismiss it as a moment of madness brought on by the fever. As she reached the door, she saw that her fears were well founded. Larten was inside and he had latched on to Yasmin's left arm. Yasmin was the mother of the baby, and Larten was feeding from her as her child did every day. But he wasn't interested in milk. He had made a cut, either with his nails or teeth, and was gulping blood from a wound far bigger than any a sane vampire would have ever made.

"Larten!" Malora screeched, trying to fake shock. "What are you doing?"

He didn't respond. His eyes were closed and he was drinking happily, ignorant of the screams, the way Yasmin and the other woman were striking him, the men trying to tug him off. He only knew blood.

As the sailors gawped, Malora looked around, spotted a bucket of water, picked it up and doused Larten. The shock of the cold water made him fall away. He tried to get up and grab the bucket, but he toppled and fell in a heap on the floor.

Yasmin ran to her husband and her baby and they barged through the sailors, wanting to get as far away from the madman as possible.

Malora knew she had to act quickly. "Help me," she snapped at two of the crew. "He's had some kind of fit. We have to take him back to his cabin."

The sailors were dubious – a fit couldn't explain the blood smeared around his lips and chin – but they liked Malora, so they picked up the almost unconscious Larten and hauled him back to his bed. Malora followed, talking rapidly, telling the others trailing behind of the medicine she'd need, asking them to apologise to Yasmin, hoping they wouldn't stop to ask questions if she kept them busy.

As the sailors manoeuvred Larten through the doorway of their cabin and into bed, Malora paused outside and offered up a silent prayer to the gods. It seemed as if they'd got away with it. The captain was arriving and he looked like thunder, but she was sure she could laugh her way out of this. She'd blame it on the flu, let them strap Larten down if they wished to stop him straying again. No real harm had been done. All things considered, it could have been a lot worse.

And then, as the captain roared at his crew and demanded to know what the hell was going on, it *did* get worse.

"He drinks blood!" someone yelled.

The captain and the others fell quiet. The sailors who'd dropped off Larten joined the rest of the crew outside and stared with them at the person who had spoken. It was, of course, young Daniel Abrams.

"He's a bloodsucker," Daniel said, relishing the attention. He hadn't meant to speak up, but the drama in the cabin had excited him and he wanted to see more fireworks. "He's some sort of demon."

"Don't be ridiculous," Malora snapped. "It's the flu. He didn't know what he was doing. Captain, you must believe me."

And maybe he would have, except that was when a chaos-craving Daniel played his ace.

"If he's not a bloodsucker, why was you cutting open sailors and bottling their blood the last place we docked? It was t' feed yer bloodthirsty beast of a master! There's vials in the cabin," he said triumphantly to the shocked captain. "Search. You'll find 'em, still bloodstained, I bet, unless he's licked 'em clean."

"Daniel!" Malora cried. "Why are you doing this? I thought you were my friend."

But Daniel had forgotten about his crush on Malora. He craved bloodshed. The scene with Yasmin had whetted his appetite and he couldn't stop now, any more than Larten could have when the hunger overwhelmed him.

The captain studied Daniel soberly, then turned his gaze on Malora. "Step out of the way, please, ma'am." He nodded at a few of his sailors.

Malora shook her head. "Captain, no, don't listen to him, it was just—"

"Ma'am!" the captain barked. "Ye're not listening t' me. Ye have t' move *now*. This is bad fer yer master and if ye don't get away from there immediately it'll be bad fer you and all. If ye give him to us, I'll settle fer that and spare ye. But if ye stand up fer him… fer what he did…" His features hardened. "It's time t' choose."

The young woman looked from one stern-faced sailor to another. There was a vicious gleam to their eyes — they had caught the same dark lust as Daniel. Her friends had disappeared and she knew better than to beg for mercy. It didn't exist here now.

Malora nodded slowly, accepting what destiny had unleashed upon her. Unlike Larten, she had no problem choosing her path. No problem at all.

"So be it," she said, softly closing the door so as not to disturb the unconscious vampire. As the sailors bunched around her, silent as a pack of sharks, she lay the palm of one hand on the door and bid a silent farewell to the lover she would never get a chance to truly love. Then, turning calmly, she faced the mob closing in on her, sneered at their savage, bestial hunger, drew a knife and made her stand.

CHAPTER
TWENTY-THREE

If the crew had stormed the cabin, Larten would not have been able to resist. He had passed out on top of his bed. It would have been a simple matter for them to turn him over, bare his left breast and drive a sharpened stake through his heart.

But superstition and fear swept through the sailors once they had dealt with Malora. Instead of rushing to finish the cruel business, they paused to debate the situation. And in that pause their doubts exploded.

"He's a vampire," one hissed, and explained what vampires were for those who didn't know. It was a maelstrom of myths, theories and hysteria after that.

"He can turn into a bat."

"He can turn into smoke and slip away."

"He's powerful at night, but weak in the day. We should wait for the sun."

"A stake through the heart will destroy him."

"So will sunlight."

"And holy water, but we ain't got any of that."

"If we attack now and he wakes, he'll be stronger than us."

"Wait."

"Daylight turns them to ash."

"Aye, wait."

"He can't hide from the sun."

"Wait."

"Aye."

"*Wait.*"

Larten was groggy when he awoke. He could have happily slept much longer, but something had disturbed him. Creaking noises, sharper and louder than the normal twangs of the ship, coming from directly overhead. As he listened, the sounds came again. It was as if the room was trying to rip itself apart.

As Larten sat up, confused, a couple of planks were torn loose from the ceiling and sunlight pierced the cabin. He flinched and drew back from the beams. There was laughter outside.

"There! He's frightened o' the light. Hurry, lads. Once we pull the rest o' that ceiling away, he's finished. He'll be ash by breakfast."

Larten stared with astonishment as a crowd of sailors hacked through the thin roof of his cabin. They were working like a team of ants. They'd tear all of the planks away in a matter of minutes and Larten would have nowhere to shelter then.

He couldn't remember much of the night before, but he swiftly worked out what had happened. They had discovered his true identity and were coming to kill him. This was serious. The sunlight wouldn't destroy him instantly, but he couldn't stay exposed to it for long. He would have to retreat and seek shelter in the bowels of the ship. He could barricade himself in somewhere, but it was going to be nigh impossible to keep them out. Still, he had to try.

"Malora?" he croaked, although he already knew she wasn't here. He looked for her, to be sure, then sighed with relief. They'd either captured her or she had gone over to their side to save her own neck. He didn't mind which, just as long as she wasn't sucked down into the pit with him. If this was to be his end, so be it, but there was no reason why the innocent girl should suffer too.

The vampire grinned bleakly as the sailors tore the ceiling to shreds. He felt better than he had in ages, stomach still warm with Yasmin's blood, head clearer than it had been for several days. Ironically, it seemed that he had got the better of the flu at last, so at least he could die in good health.

Larten washed his hands in a finger bowl, gargled from a glass of water then drank the rest. He dusted off his clothes, brushed his hair back and blew his nose several times for good measure. Vampires didn't fear death. Larten had already lived longer than most humans. This would be a good way to die, hunted and staked by a mob. Seba would chuckle proudly if word ever reached him in Vampire Mountain. "When you have to go," he had often said to Larten and Wester, "try to go in style!"

As the last of the ceiling was prised away with crowbars, Larten crouched, then sprang through the gap that had been created, landing on the deck like a cat. The sailors cried out with alarm and reeled away from the freed vampire. As they scrambled over one another, shrieking with terror, Larten stood to his full height and glared at his tormentors, looking majestic despite his dirty clothes, red eyes and scraggly beard.

"Come then, humans!" he bellowed. "I am Larten Crepsley of the vampire clan and I fear no man."

The sailors paused and gawped. They hadn't expected a response like this. They thought he'd howl and screech and fight like a cornered rat to the bitter, bloody end. But here he stood, tall and straight, unafraid of his foes, challenging them to do their worst.

The captain recovered and pointed at Larten with a hook he'd kept over his bed for many years in case he ever faced a mutiny. "Crosses!" he barked and six sailors pressed forward holding crucifixes.

Larten laughed. Perhaps the clan didn't require Bram Stoker to spread silly myths about the creatures of the night. These humans had accepted the old, crazy legends without any need of a novel.

The captain scowled. He didn't like the way the monster was laughing. The beast should be cowering, begging them to spare his worthless life. The captain was eager to finish off the vampire, but first he wanted to see that smirk wiped from the villain's face.

"Ye think this is funny?" the captain snarled.

"I think it is pathetic," Larten retorted.

"Ye're a monster. A vampire. A servant o' the devil himself."

"You know far more about the devil than I do, sir," Larten replied. He wouldn't normally have played for time – it would have made more sense to make his break and seek shelter from the sun – but he was scanning the crowd for Malora. He wanted to be sure she was safe before he fled. Maybe curse her as a traitor or act as if he'd fooled her along with the rest, to make them think she hadn't been working in league with him.

The captain saw Larten looking and realised what he was searching for. A dark flicker of a smile danced across his lips. "Are ye worried about yer wench?" he asked innocently.

Larten felt a chill form inside his stomach. "She knows nothing about me," he said, trying to distance himself from Malora to help her as much as he could — if that was still possible. "She is just a girl I picked up and used. I do not care what you do with her."

"That's good," the captain purred. "Then ye won't be too upset when ye look up and see *that*." He pointed to the rigging with his hook.

The last thing Larten wanted to do was raise his gaze. He knew what was waiting for him if he did. But a vampire of good standing never tries to hide from the truth, and Larten had been trained always to face his fears and losses.

It was a bright day and his eyes were narrow slits against the painful rays of the sun. But he could see the sails clearly enough, and the wooden rigging to which they were attached. And he could also see poor Malora hanging from one of the poles, a length of rope looped around her neck, swaying lifelessly in the breeze and from the ever-constant rise and fall of the ship.

A cold calm washed through Larten Crepsley. Many years earlier, as a boy, he had experienced a similar calmness just before he'd killed the brute of a man who had murdered his best friend. It was as if he withdrew emotionally from the world. He forgot every rule he'd lived by and every moral restraint he had ever placed upon himself.

In that moment he was neither man nor vampire, but a force, one that would not stop until it had been spent. In the factory he'd only had one man to direct his fury against. Here he had dozens. And for that he was glad.

"They used to call me Quicksilver," he whispered, smiling hollowly. "Fastest hands in the world."

Then the smile vanished. His eyes flashed. And like a sliver of deadly mercury, he attacked.

CHAPTER
TWENTY-FOUR

Larten sat near the prow of the ship. He was holding the baby and absentmindedly bouncing it up and down. The baby was cooing happily. Larten's hands were soaked with blood and the red, sticky liquid had seeped through the baby's shawl, but neither seemed to notice or care.

He would never recall the slaughter in detail. Fragments would haunt him, both awake and sleeping, for the rest of his life. Faces would flash in front of him or shimmer in the theatre of his dreams. He'd see his nails, jagged and deadly, slicing open a throat as if it was a slab of butter. His fingers, gripping a man's skull, digging deep, crushing bone, sinking into brain.

Sometimes he'd get a strange taste in his mouth. It always puzzled him for a few seconds. Then he would remember biting off a sailor's salty toes while the man was alive, leaving him a while, then returning to finish the job like a butcher who had been momentarily sidetracked.

He had saved the captain for last, letting him bear witness to the destruction. The seasoned sailor wept and begged for his men's lives, then for his own. Larten only grinned and pointed to the girl dangling above their heads.

In his dreams he often chased sailors into the rigging. In reality only three had tried to climb to safety, but in Larten's nightmares there were hundreds and the poles stretched to the sky and beyond. But no matter how many fled ahead of him, he always killed every last one of them before he stirred and woke.

The baby gurgled, then started to cry hungrily. Larten bounced him a few more times, hoping to shush him, but the infant boy wasn't to be distracted. With a sigh, Larten reluctantly turned from the prow and surveyed the deck of corpses.

He knew it would be bad, but this was even worse than he'd feared. So many hacked (*bitten, chewed, torn*) to pieces. Blood everywhere. Guts hanging from the ropes in the rigging. Heads set on spikes and hooks. The eyes of one were missing, two crosses rammed deep into the bloody sockets.

Larten had seen much in his time on the battlefields of the world, but nothing as vicious as this. He wanted to weep, but he could find no tears within himself. It would have been hypocritical to cry. He didn't deserve that release.

Steeling himself, Larten stared long and hard at the bodies. This was *his* work. He could blame it on the flu, but that would be a lie. He had chosen to do this. Malora had been murdered and he had let himself go wild and wreak a terrible revenge. He felt shame and disgust, more than he could ever express. There was no justification and no hiding. *He* did this. He had become the monster these people feared. Paris had warned him of the dangers of indecision and isolation, but he had ignored the Prince's advice. This was the result. This was what happened when vampires went bad.

Larten picked his way through the mess, holding the baby high above it, glad that the child was too young to understand any of this. Entering the boy's cabin, he found a small bottle half full of milk. Sitting on the bed, he perched the baby on his lap and let him feed.

It was only as the baby greedily gulped the milk that Larten wondered what had happened to the boy's mother.

When the child had drunk his fill, Larten scoured the ship from top to bottom, praying he'd find the pretty Yasmin alive, cowering in a corner. If he could hand her back her baby, he would have done at least that much right on this awful, notorious day.

But Yasmin was nowhere on board. He found the body of the other woman, along with the corpses of the male passengers, mixed in with the remains of the sailors, but Yasmin must have leapt overboard, preferring the sea to death by the vampire's wretched hands.

Or else he had thrown her off.

Until the night he died, Larten would pray a few times a week, begging the gods to reveal Yasmin's end to him. It seemed important, a crucial missing piece of the puzzle. Until he put it in place he could never draw a line under the calamity. But as hard as he prayed, that memory would always be a mystery to him.

What he did find during his search was a sealed door. It had been locked from the outside. The key was missing, but to Larten – *Quicksilver*, he'd told them, as if by using a different name he could distance himself from the guilt – it was a simple thing to pick. Moments later he pushed the door open and four terrified pairs of eyes stared out at him.

One of the four was a high-ranking mate. Larten immediately understood why he had spared this man — even in his murderous rage, he'd known that he would need someone to steer the ship. Right now Larten didn't care if he lived or died, but a part of him had been thinking about life, even while he was dealing out death to all in sight.

But what of the others? There were two men and the boy, Daniel Abrams. Why had he let these live? It couldn't have been mercy or because he needed them for the ship — he would have spared another mate, not a worthless boy, if that was the case. So why...?

The answer came to him and he chuckled drily.

He'd had to keep a few alive. The deck was awash with blood, but it would soon spoil and be of no use to him. He had to assume that they were a long way from land. He might be on this ship a good while yet. He would need to feed.

Still chuckling – edgily now, the laughter threatening to turn into a scream – he shut the door on the moaning, weeping humans, locked it, then retired to the deck with the baby, to wet his whistle before the pools of blood thickened and soured in the sun.

Having drunk his fill on deck, Larten retreated from the daylight before it burnt him. He didn't care what happened to him now, but if he gave in to bloodthirsty insanity or let himself die, the baby would perish too.

Larten cradled the boy in the shelter of the captain's cabin, holding him gently as if he was something precious. Nothing would ever set right this dreadful wrong, but if he could protect this innocent child, that would be one less dark mark against his name when he passed from this world of hurt and shame. He felt as far from the gates of Paradise as it was possible to get, so it wasn't redemption that he sought. He simply didn't want to add to his crimes, even though in the greater scheme of things one more wouldn't make any real difference.

He changed the baby's undergarments when he realised why the boy had started crying again. Then he went below deck to find more milk and look for other food.

They slept in the cabin that night, the baby tucked between Larten and the wall. But although the boy snoozed sweetly, Larten spent most of the night staring at the ceiling. It wasn't because he had become accustomed to sleeping in the day or because of the baby's surprisingly deep snoring, but because after what he'd done, he couldn't face the nightmares that were certain to be lying in wait for him.

Shortly before dawn, after feeding the baby again, Larten returned to the room with the four captives and opened the door. They thought he'd come to kill them and they cowered against the wall. But he only pointed a finger at the senior mate and said, "You."

The sailor crossed himself, muttered a quick prayer, then staggered out of the cabin. He was sweating and trembling, but otherwise carried himself with dignity.

Larten locked the door and led the way to the deck. The mate's face blanched when he cast his eye around, but he didn't try to run.

"You can sail this ship?" Larten asked wearily. If not for the baby, he'd have lowered himself over the side and gone for a swim with the sharks. But if the boy was to live, this had to be done.

"I'm no captain," the mate said quietly.

"If we are to live, you will have to be," Larten retorted.

"If I had a crew…"

"You do not. Can you steer it anyway?"

The mate checked the rigging and shrugged. "We're not so far from land — a week's sailing, I reckon. I can get us there if the weather holds. We'll struggle t' dock, but we can get close enough t' set one o' the scows down and row ashore. *If* the weather holds. If we hit a storm, we're finished."

Larten nodded. "Do your best. I will be taking care of the child. If you need me, shout. Do not try and release the others, and do not try to kill me — I will hear you coming, even in my sleep. If you can drop us ashore, I will set you free."

"What about them?" the mate called as Larten left. He pointed a shaking finger at the corpses. "They'll fester if we leave 'em. The stench..."

"I will dispose of them later," Larten promised. "When the sun goes down. That is when I am most powerful, is it not?" Smiling thinly, he went inside to play with the baby, leaving the mate to steer the ship of corpses through the waves of the ever-hungry sea that would soon receive their lifeless, bloodied hulks.

CHAPTER
TWENTY-FIVE

Feeding the baby and prisoners became the focus of Larten's time. Daniel and the sailors were easy to care for – he just threw them food and water a couple of times a day – but the baby was a different matter. Larten had no experience of babies and was astonished by how often the child wanted to feed. Keeping the boy content was a full-time job.

The mate in charge of the ship reported to Larten regularly. Larten had no interest in their course – he wouldn't have cared if they'd sailed in circles forever – but it was easier to let the mate deliver his reports and nod thoughtfully while pretending to listen.

Larten was ravenous – he needed blood – but he waited until the mate said they were a day from shore. Tucking in the baby, he went below to the locked room and opened the door. Daniel and the sailors thought that he was coming to feed them and they shuffled forward eagerly. They still feared the vampire, but had come to believe that he meant them no harm.

Not wishing to alarm them, Larten moved quickly, as he had when he'd embarked on his killing spree. Darting from one to the other, he blew a sharp breath of gas in their faces, the gas of the vampires that sent humans to sleep. Once they were unconscious he drank from each of them, then refilled the vials which, unknown to him, had cost Malora her life.

Daniel stirred as Larten was leaving. The vampire had breathed on the boy last, so Daniel hadn't been dealt as strong a blast of the gas as the others. Larten took no notice as the boy's eyes flickered open, only closed the door and locked it, then went to feed the baby.

Larten spent most of that last night on deck, watching by the light of the stars as they drew closer to land, thinking of what he'd done, numbly considering what he must do next. He didn't know much about Greenland, but he knew it was an ice-covered, sparsely populated country. It had many cold, lonely, unforgiving places where a vampire could pass quietly from this world. He would find a suitably desolate spot and let the snow and ice finish him off. A fittingly meek finale for a vampire who had lost the right to die a noble death.

The mate approached late the following evening, as

Larten was feeding the baby. "We're almost there," he noted.

"Aye," Larten murmured.

"We should make port not long after sunset, if the wind's fair."

"I will disembark before that," Larten said.

The mate frowned. "Disembark?"

"I will take a scow and sail ashore by myself."

"Are ye sure?" the mate asked. "There's nothing much along this stretch and the weather's fierce inhospitable."

"Good," Larten said shortly.

A wave of joy swept through the sailor. He had tried not to think about what would happen when they docked, but whenever he did, he saw no way that the vampire would let them live. They were witnesses to the massacre. He surely could not spare them if he wanted to escape.

But now the mate saw that Larten didn't care. He was going ashore to die. For the first time in a week, the sailor faced the future with real hope. He almost cried, he was so relieved.

"You will take care of the child when I go?" Larten asked.

"Of course. I'll take him home with me. I have six already, so one more won't make much difference."

"Thank you," Larten said softly. "And," he added as the mate returned to the wheel, "you will keep him away from vampires?"

The sailor nodded grimly. "Aye, sir. That I most definitely will."

The mate helped Larten ready and lower the scow. Before he departed, Larten went down to the locked room one last time to release the prisoners. He could have left that job to the mate, but he wanted to do it himself, so they could come up, see him leave and know for certain that they had nothing to fear from this night on.

"Come, gentlemen," Larten said as he opened the door. "Your time of captivity is over. You are free to…"

He came to a stunned, horrified stop.

Daniel Abrams was sitting on the floor, hands and lips as red with blood as Larten's had been a week before. The boy had torn open the throats of the two men while they were unconscious and drank as much of their blood as he could stomach. He'd even bitten chunks out of their flesh and eaten it. He was chewing a sliver of cheek, pausing every so often to spit out blood, when Larten entered.

Daniel's face lit up crazily when he spotted the

vampire and he staggered to his feet. "I'm one o' yer lot now," he cackled, waving the strip of flesh at Larten as if it was a flag. "Ye don't have t' kill me. Ye can take me with ye. I'm a bloodsucker too, see? We're the same."

Larten stared at the boy, first with shock, then disgust. "You think that you are the same as me?" he snarled.

"Aye," the boy hooted. "We both kill and drink blood. What's the difference?"

And the awful thing was, he was right. When you put the two of them side by side, there was no real difference at all. A pair of well-matched monsters.

Larten backed out of the room, away from the blinking, spitting, blood-smeared boy. He glanced at the murdered sailors, then bolted for the deck, where he raced to the side and threw up over the railing. Before Daniel Abrams could climb the steps and ask again to travel with him, Larten ducked into the captain's cabin and picked up the baby.

He had meant to bid the child farewell, but as he stared at the chubby babe, he decided he couldn't leave the boy behind. Not with a beast like Daniel Abrams on the prowl. Maybe they *were* cut from the same cloth, but at least Larten wouldn't feed on the innocent baby. If Larten took him from the ship, the boy was doomed, but death in the wilds was preferable to what might happen to the infant if he remained.

Larten never considered the possibility of simply killing Daniel. In a mindless panic, he thought that there were only two options — take the baby or leave him to be bled and devoured.

Larten wrapped the child up warmly and staggered across the deck to the scow. The mate was bewildered when he saw the wild-eyed vampire climb in with the baby. "What are you doing?" he shouted. "I thought you were leaving him."

But Larten would neither listen nor respond. Before the mate could stop him, he cast off and rowed madly towards the icy shore. Understanding would come to the sailor later, when he discovered the young cannibal below, but for the time being he could only stand on deck and stare dumbly at the swiftly receding boat.

Larten thrust ahead without pause, muscles aching, neck bent stiffly, never looking up. If he'd gone in the wrong direction and missed land, perhaps he would have rowed until he weakened and died. But the mate had pointed the scow true and before long he struck shore and ground to a halt.

Larten stood in a daze and gazed at a giant sheet of

ice that seemed to stretch from one end of the horizon to the other. For a moment he was overwhelmed and thought about returning to the ship. Then he grinned darkly, seeing the obstacle for what any true vampire would have judged it — a challenge to be met.

Picking up the baby, Larten strapped the silent, shivering boy to his back and made sure he was secure. Then, with a cry of total abandon, he leapt from the boat and cut a path towards the glittering wall of ice. Dragging his way through mounds of thigh-high snow, Larten laughed manically at the moon and stars as he pushed on in delirious pursuit of his place in that other, eternal, always freezing night.

To be continued …

BOOK THREE

PALACE OF
THE DAMNED

COMING OCTOBER 2011

**You've reached the end...
now go back to the beginning.**

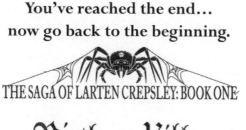

THE SAGA OF LARTEN CREPSLEY: BOOK ONE

Birth of a Killer

Out now in paperback.

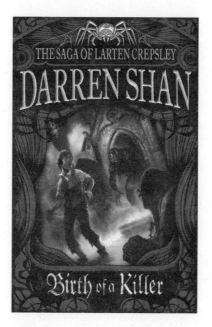

When terrible events force young Larten Crespley to flee his home he finds himself alone in the world. Then he meets the mysterious Seba Nile, who introduces him to the ways of the vampire clan. Travelling with Seba, Larten experiences the adventures he has always dreamed about. But will he turn his back on humanity and join a world from which there can be no return...?

THE SAGA OF DARREN SHAN

Cirque Du Freak
A LIVING NIGHTMARE

The Vampire's Assistant
THE NIGHTMARE CONTINUES

Tunnels of Blood
WHERE DEATH STALKS THE DARKNESS

Vampire Mountain
HOME OF THE DAMNED

Trials of Death
THE BLOODLETTING BEGINS

The Vampire Prince
WHO WILL RULE THE NIGHT...?

Hunters of the Dusk
VAMPIRES AT WAR

Allies of the Night
OLD FACES - NEW NIGHTMARES

Killers of the Dawn
THE HUNTERS BECOME THE HUNTED

The Lake of Souls
FISH FOR THE DEAD

Lord of the Shadows
OF IS DESTRUCTION

Sons of Destiny
THE FINAL ACT

THE DEMONATA